WEEKS PUBLIC LIBRARY
GREENLAND, N.H.

Chapter One

As the sun set, the temperature dropped. The rain, which had been falling steadily all day, turned to sleet. Zachary pulled the damp edge of his hoodie across his face to shield it from ice pellets and hunched his shoulders against the wind. Charlie's house was on this street, it had to be. But nothing here looked familiar and the specter of doubt that had been haunting him since he left began to speak.

It whispered that Charlie wouldn't remember him, wouldn't help him. It warned him to give up.

He swiped at his runny nose with the back of his sleeve. Grabbing the strap of his backpack, he shifted its weight to the other shoulder. A few things inside were wrapped in plastic grocery bags that he'd scavenged along the way, but most weren't. His pack felt heavier than when he left, so everything was probably either soaked or ruined. At least he'd thought to dump his school books before he left.

Charlie's house was on the edge of town—*that* he remembered. The house had a big yard, thick with trees, and Zachary thought he could find it. But outside of town the distance between streetlights became wider, and the light dimmed, making landmarks harder to find. He thought he recognized one cedar tree as the furthest point Charlie had allowed him to ride his bike one summer, but there were so many trees now that he couldn't be sure.

Zachary sifted through his dusty memories of Charlie's house, the last one on a narrow street. Overhead, tree branches intertwined, he remembered, filtering the summer's sunlight and leaving dappled shadows on the sandy lane below. It was peaceful there, and quiet. Crickets chirping at night lulled him to sleep, and the surf's rumbling woke him in the morning.

Zachary looked at the street before him. Nothing was recognizable, nothing was the same. The specter began to stir but he pushed it away with the last of his strength. The rain was so cold and he was so tired. Somehow, he'd thought this would be easier

Gusty wind pushed pellets of sleet through an unprotected gap in his hoodie. They melted against his neck, the icy water trickling down his spine. With a violent shiver, he tightened the grip on his hood, adjusting his shoulders so the cold fabric would hang away from his body. His jeans were already soaked through, and his sneakers were heavy with water.

He needed to get out of this weather.

Objects in front of him started to blur, coming in and out of focus as if he were walking under water. If he went back to the beach stairs he could wrap himself in the tarp he'd left wedged behind the rock and try again tomorrow. But that would mean another day hidden under the stairs, avoiding notice. Shifting the weight of his back-pack, he forced himself to stay awake.

One more street.

One more street before letting the weather force him to stop for another night. With a breath that tugged at his chest, he trudged down the lane, following the trail of flickering yellow light from the streetlights.

This last house might be Charlie's. The front porch looked familiar: deep and shaded. Flanking a picture window was a pair of blue Adirondack chairs very like the ones that Charlie built and painted. On warm summer afternoons, he and Charlie would settle into chairs on the porch, watching the daylight fade to gold and the slow descent of the sun. They listened for the first chirp of crickets, and when the deep croak of frogs followed, it was time to get ready for bed. The house looked very much like Charlie's, but it seemed smaller.

Older.

Across the street, from under the relative shelter of a grove of cedar trees, Zachary watched for movement inside the house, careful to stay in the shadows. He would recognize Charlie, even after five years.

Inside, the house was dark. Charlie always kept one lamp in the front window lit until he went to bed. Twice a week, when Inlet Beach's community newspaper was published, Charlie would extend his green recliner and stretch out, reading under the warm glow of that lamp. Those nights, instead of sitting on the porch, Zachary played quietly on the floor with his wooden blocks and construction trucks. That slice of the day, after supper and before bedtime was what Charlie called "a man's reward for a full day of work". And it was Zachary's favorite.

At Charlie's house a man could relax. There was no anger or shouting, no drinking or hitting. There was food in the house and Zachary slept peacefully, all night long. At Charlie's house, Zachary could let his guard down.

Overhead the wind howled. In the distance a tree branch snapped, crashing to the ground. Zachary startled and looked up. The streetlights swayed in the wind, their spotlight flickering on the wet pavement of the road. Drawing his shoulders to his ears to block the wind, he dug his fingers into his armpits and shivered. He was quickly running out of choices. Unable to shake the chill he had picked up sleeping unsheltered in the woods the first night, he didn't think it was a good idea to sleep outside again. But the thought of retracing his steps, walking into town to sleep under dripping beach stairs was almost too much to bear.

Coming out of the shadows, Zachary approached the little blue house. Over the porch, a gutter overflowed, splattering water onto the wooden railing below. Not something Charlie would have allowed to happen.

Climbing the stairs slowly, one by one, he tried to look in the window, but it was too dark. Wiping his runny nose with his damp sleeve, he cupped his hands over his forehead and leaned against the picture window. The same blue couch where Zachary sometimes napped spanned the far wall. The long coffee table with the narrow drawers might still contain the treasures Zachary gathered from the beach.

Zachary exhaled. Charlie's house. It was going to be okay.

When Charlie opened the door, Zachary would offer the firm, confident handshake that Charlie had taught him. They would talk and Charlie would fix everything.

Charlie always made everything all right.

Releasing his pack, he felt it hit the floor beside him with a dull thud. Zachary pushed the hood from his head and knocked on the door. A gust of wind slammed against the house, scattering leaves and spitting rain. He turned, angling his body away from the wind. Dark water squished from his shoes and a patch of icy fabric from his shirt touched his skin, sending a shock of cold into his core. He gasped at the pain.

Another knock, and still no sound from inside the house. Swallowing past the lump in his throat, he fought the whispers that said Charlie would *never* answer the door because he had moved away. Five years was a long time to be away and he couldn't expect Charlie to be here waiting for him.

An idea presented itself--something Charlie used to tell him--and it brought a hint of a smile to Zachary's face. Slinging his pack over his shoulder, he leapt from the porch and raced to the back of the house. Charlie used to tell him that front door was for company, but the back door is where friends came to visit.

Charlie could be inside right now, with the lights off, as a test to see if Zachary had remembered what he had been taught. And he did. He did remember. Zachary remembered everything Charlie ever said.

Using all of his energy and the last of his hope, Zachary jumped onto the back step with such force that he almost crashed into the door. Righting himself, he flicked the rain from his bangs and allowed himself the barest of smiles, the first since he left almost a week ago.

He knocked. Then, with his breathing jagged and heavy in his ears, he waited. Any minute, Charlie would come. Zachary would have a hot shower, warm clothes, and someone to listen to him.

Zachary glanced at the backyard, welcoming the memories of the summers he'd spent here when he was little. At the end of the gravel driveway was a detached garage where Charlie kept his truck. At the end of the day, it was Zachary's responsibility to help unload the tools and sweep the truck bed. A clean truck and an organized jobsite demonstrated respect for both the clients and the job at hand.

On Sunday afternoons they listened to the Mariners game on a tinny AM radio while Charlie checked his tools and Zachary washed his bike, both of them getting ready for the week ahead. Zachary wondered if Charlie still checked his tools or if his bike was still in the garage.

He'd have to ask.

Another knock at the back door, this time louder. The wind roared overhead and the rain lashed at the cedar shingles, but inside the house was still.

No one was coming to the door.

Holding his breath, he pulled the sleeve of his hoodie tight across his fist and punched a hole in the small window on the door. Carefully reaching through the jagged glass, he flipped the deadbolt, opened the door, and entered Charlie's house.

The first job was to collect the shards of glass from the floor, and he did, sweeping the splinters into a dustpan and placing them in the garbage can, careful the edges didn't tear the plastic liner.

Only after replacing the dustpan properly behind the garbage can would he let himself rest. Sliding a chair from under the breakfast table, he allowed himself to sink into it. Crossing his arms on the smooth wooden surface, he put his head down and willed the room to stop spinning. Beads of perspiration gathered on his forehead and waves of nausea rolled in his stomach, but he forced them back. He would not be sick in Charlie's house.

He woke to the sound of the furnace register pinging and the tickle of warm air blowing across his ankle. While he was asleep, rain water had dripped from his clothes and puddled on Charlie's hardwood floor. Charlie had laid that floor himself when he built this house and Zachary didn't intend to damage it. Rising unsteadily from the chair, he opened the back door to a blast of icy wind. Gritting his teeth, he stepped out to the porch and stripped to his underwear, draping his wet clothes over the railing. Then he made his way to the bathroom and started a hot shower.

The first shock of hot water burned his icy skin, but Zachary forced himself to stay under the spray until the water turned cold. If he thought this shower would be enough to warm him, he was wrong. With chattering teeth, he steeled himself against another wave of dizziness. As he leaned against the shower wall to steady himself, he realized he had no dry clothes. Hoping Charlie would understand, he went into the closet, selected the warmest clothes he could find and layered them over his body.

They smelled like Charlie, the clothes. A mixture of spicy aftershave, freshly cut wood, and a tiny bit of lavender. That made Zachary smile, too. One summer Colleen convinced Charlie to add lavender fabric softener to his laundry, insisting he would like it. He did, and he added softener to every load after that, declaring that "if a man's going to work hard all day, at least his clothes should be comfortable and smell nice." A surge of longing for the man who used to make everything better tugged at Zachary's heart, but he pushed it away. Sentimentality was distracting, and he didn't have time for it.

As he slipped Charlie's socks over his cold feet, another wave of dizziness hit him but this time he lost his balance, dropping to the floor like a sandbag. Squeezing his hands into fists, he laid his head on the floor and waited for the sensation to pass.

A memory flashed before him, taking advantage of his distraction, forcing him to remember the last day of fourth grade. As he tucked his favorite beach shorts into his suitcase, his mother casually announced that he wasn't going to spend summers at Inlet Beach with Charlie anymore. The drop off was inconvenient, she said, and Charlie didn't seem grateful. No matter how much Zachary cried, she wouldn't relent. Zachary never forgave her, and he never asked her for anything else. But he didn't think she even noticed.

Scrubbing his face with his fingers to chase away the memory, Zachary rose unsteadily and left the bedroom. It would not do to have Charlie find him asleep.

Making his way back to the kitchen, he glanced at the clock, surprised at how late it was. Charlie went to bed at exactly ten o'clock, and it was almost midnight. Where could he be?

Desperation gnawed at him, but Zachary pushed it away. Charlie would come back, he would. Didn't he always tell Zachary that Inlet Beach was the most beautiful place on earth? Except for trips to the lumberyard, there wasn't really any reason to leave. So of course Charlie would come home. Zachary just needed to keep himself busy until he did.

He looked around the kitchen for something to do.

Soup.

Soup would be a good idea. Zachary hadn't eaten a hot meal since he left, and soup would make him warm. He could make enough for two and keep the leftovers for Charlie, in case he was cold, when he came home.

Pulling open the cabinet door, he felt an unexpected spark of pride when he realized he didn't need to climb on a kitchen chair to reach the soup pot inside the top cabinet anymore. Charlie would like that.

Chapter Two

Officer Arnold Bushwick rolled his patrol car to a stop across from Charlie Gimball's house and switched off the headlights. The silent alarm inside the house had tripped and even though it might be a gust of wind from the storm, Arnold wanted to investigate.

Charlie's house was on the outskirts of town, tucked under a canopy of old cedar trees. Charlie said that he knew where the ocean is, having lived all of his eighty years at Inlet Beach, but he preferred the smell of the forest and rustle of the leaves to the commotion of town.

Unhooking his radio from the receiver, Arnold called into the station. "Carl, I'm on site but it looks quiet. Any response to phone calls?"

Despite the storm and the number of calls coming into the station when he left, the response was immediate. "We've called twice, no answer."

"I'm going in."

There had been trouble a few years ago, with kids breaking into vacation homes and destroying them, using them for party houses. The gangs chose houses that were remote, away from neighbors who might report activity. A few years ago, the Jensen house on the bluff had been invaded and ruined in a very short time. It took months to repair that house, and Arnold blamed himself for not catching it sooner. A mistake he wouldn't repeat.

Arnold reached under the seat and pulled out his flashlight. He'd been to Charlie's house several times, and he remembered the layout: one floor with a wide porch spanning the front and a smaller deck out back. Two bedrooms on the left, living room in the front, and kitchen in the back. A detached garage sat at the bottom of the driveway for his truck and tools.

Pushing the car door against the wind, Arnold got out and let the wind slam it behind him. The house was dark, but seemed undisturbed.

He moved closer.

A sudden blast of wind pushed through the tree branches, bringing with it jagged balls of sleet and a shower of pine needles. Arnold turned up his collar and hunched his shoulders. This storm was stronger than predicted, and he hoped it would end quickly. Visitors in town for Christmas week might appreciate the show, but he never liked the chaos that followed a storm.

Switching on the light, Arnold cupped the beam against his palm to dim it and crossed the narrow street to the house. He heard the water overflowing the gutter before he saw it. A river of water burst from a seam in the gutter, pounding the wooden railing and flooding the floor below. Charlie would have heard and fixed that, no matter what time it was.

A shiver of warning touched the back of his neck. He'd always been uneasy about Charlie's living alone this far from town.

Arnold silenced his radio and followed the stone path to the house, the mud squishing beneath the slate as he walked. Shining the light on the porch, Arnold checked for signs of a break-in. Both chairs on the porch were undisturbed, and the picture window to the right of the door was intact. Directing the beam between the railing slats and behind the chairs, Arnold found nothing out of place.

What was on the steps made him hesitate: a clear trail of footprints led to the front door. Wet and flecked with mud, they were fresh, maybe an hour or two old. They stopped at the front door, suggesting Charlie may have let the visitor in but that didn't seem possible.

Charlie didn't answer the front door and never stayed up this late.

Reaching for his radio, Arnold adjusted the volume and called into the station. "I'm on site. Nothing's out of place, but things seem 'off'. I'm going to check the back."

The radio crackled and Carl replied. "We've gotten a few calls about storm damage while you've been gone and things are getting hectic. Come back as soon as you can."

"Roger."

A quick check of the front door showed no sign of forced entry — the lock was intact, the wood undamaged. A glance into the house through the picture window showed nothing unusual inside. A twist of the doorknob confirmed that the house was locked. If the back door was locked as well, it would have to be called in as a false alarm. In the morning, when his shift ended, Arnold could drive by and check the house again.

The slate path led around the house to the back door. A sliver of light from the kitchen slowed his steps, but the clothes draped over the railing stopped him in his tracks. Charlie wore red flannel shirts and brown construction pants. It was one of the staples of life at Inlet Beach. The wet clothes on the railing were definitely not Charlie's.

Arnold reached toward his belt and unsnapped the safety hood from his gun. Thirty years on the force at Inlet Beach and he had yet to fire his gun in the line of duty, a fact for which he was grateful. However, if the safety of a resident was threatened, he would not hesitate to use whatever force was necessary.

He stayed out of sight as he approached the back door. The glass window above the doorknob was smashed, its edges jagged in the frame.

Someone stood in front of the stove, his form lit only by a single bulb on the range hood. Even though the figure was angled away from the door, Arnold knew it wasn't Charlie. The intruder was tall and lanky, where Charlie was shorter and dense.

Entering the kitchen quickly, Arnold curled his fingers around the grip of his gun but didn't remove it from his belt. "Stop what you're doing and turn around."

The intruder spun around. A metal spoon clattered against the stovetop and fell to the floor. He was young, close to six feet tall but no more than a hundred and forty pounds. His eyes widened with surprise, he wore oversized clothes that looked strangely like Charlie's.

Maybe Arnold was wrong. Maybe this boy was a guest of Charlie's, but that wouldn't explain the broken window.

Releasing the grip of his gun, Arnold flicked the light switch.

The boy blinked in the sudden light, his body swaying ever so slightly. Wet hair plastered to his forehead, a trail of acne scattered across his cheeks and chin, he could not have been more than thirteen or fourteen years old.

"What's your name and where is Charlie?"

The boy narrowed his eyes as if he didn't understand the question.

Arnold's deepened his voice and spoke with authority. "I will ask you just once more: who are you, and where is Charlie?"

The boy blinked.

Arnold moved closer. The boy's eyes were glazed and unfocused. His face flushed.

Drugs.

In one fluid movement Arnold pulled the handcuffs from his belt and secured one of them around the boy's wrist. Jerking a heavy chair from under the table, he shoved the boy down into the seat. Threading the chain through the spindles, he locked the other bracelet around the boy's wrist.

With the delinquent safely restrained,

Arnold turned off the stove and reached toward his shoulder for his radio. "Carl, this is Arnold. I've confirmed a break in. One known intruder, restrained. Going to secure the area."

Arnold positioned his gun underneath the flashlight. He walked through Charlie's house, looking behind every door, in every closet, under every surface, but with every step he wished he were somewhere else. He did not want to be the one to find Charlie if something had happened to him.

When the house was secured, Arnold walked though a second time, looking for anything that might hint at Charlie's whereabouts. Or anything obviously missing, anything that punk in the kitchen may have stolen.

As he made his way back to the kitchen, he noticed none of the violence associated with the other break-ins. Nothing destroyed. Nothing missing. This break-in seemed almost apologetic. Only a small pane of glass above the lock was broken and the absence of glass on the floor suggested it had been cleaned up. Stranger still was that the intruder appeared to be freshly showered and was heating soup.

Drug kids didn't warm soup.

Arnold approached the boy. "Are you on drugs?"

The boy blinked slowly, his body swayed. "No."

"What is your name?"

He drew a long breath. "Zachary Wallofski"

"What are you doing here?" Arnold spit the questions like tacks.

Zachary sagged against his chair. "I don't know."

Arnold loathed belligerence. This punk broke into Charlie's house, stole his clothes and his food, and now refused to answer questions. What would have happened to Charlie if he had been here? At eighty-one years old, Arnold doubted Charlie could have put up much of a fight and that thought razed his patience.

A gust of wind caught the back door and slammed it shut, rattling the door jam and startling them both. It was time to leave. This mess could be unraveled at the station.

"You need to come with me. Get your stuff." Arnold rested his hand on the boy's shoulder to remove the cuffs, and froze.

Heat radiated through the boy's clothes. His breathing was ragged and his eyes unfocused.

Fever.

This boy wasn't high, he was sick. How could he have missed that? After securing the safety hood across his gun, Arnold sorted his options. The firehouse in town had medical supplies and the firemen had EMT training. They would come if Arnold called, but it would be faster if he brought the boy to them.

He asked dispatch to alert the station and quickly taped the broken window against the storm.

After releasing Zachary from the cuffs, he snapped them back onto his belt. This boy wasn't a threat; he was barely conscious.

"Let's go." Arnold softened his voice but it still echoed in the stillness of the kitchen.

Zachary obeyed without comment, shoulders slumped, steps heavy, as if he had done this before. As if this was inevitable.

After securing the back door, Arnold scooped up Zachary's backpack and carried it to the patrol car, because it didn't look like the boy could manage on his own.

As he helped Zachary navigate the muddy path to the car, Arnold couldn't shake the feeling that he knew this boy from somewhere, but nothing came to mind.

With Zachary settled into the back seat, Arnold opened the trunk to pull out the blanket he used for emergencies. If the boy had a fever, he was certainly cold as well. When he unfolded it, the blanket released a scent of lavender fabric softener and Arnold rolled his eyes. Somehow Colleen had gotten to it and washed it again, even though the entire squad had tried to explain that it wasn't professional to wrap criminals in soft scented blankets.

Chapter Three

Gordon poked a burning log with the iron and watched it collapse, the embers dropping from the grate into the bed of ash below. A splatter of rain and sleet hit the outside wall with enough force to make him investigate. Usually winter storms didn't bother him. He'd lived more than half his life at Inlet Beach, and he'd seen quite a few, but this one was different. It made him restless and on guard, as if something was about to happen.

Pushing the curtain aside, Gordon looked down to the main shopping street of Inlet Beach and frowned. Great sheets of wind and sleet blew in from the ocean and slammed against storefronts. Ropes of Christmas garland that had been carefully lit and draped across shop awnings just after Thanksgiving had been clawed away by the wind. The wrought iron garbage can at the top of the alley, the one so heavy that no one bothered to chain it down, was gone entirely.

Away from the warmth of the fireplace, the room was surprisingly cold. Gordon shivered and pulled the zipper of his fleece to his neck. Maybe he should turn up the heat in case they lost power overnight. This storm was worse than the forecasters had predicted, and in the morning, clean-up would be a community effort, especially with the Christmas Lights Festival just two days away. He laid another log on the fire and pulled a down blanket from the storage trunk. He tossed it onto the couch just as Tyra emerged from her office.

She offered him a weary smile. "Finished."

Hooking his arm around her shoulders, Gordon pulled Tyra closer and kissed the top of her head. "So we have all next week free with your family?" He added a smile in case his words didn't sound sincere.

It wasn't that he didn't like Tyra's sister, Maureen and her family, or Tyra's sister Lydia, and her dog Mulligan, he did. He liked all of them. He even looked forward to the chaos that he knew would fill the week. It's just that lately, he found himself hoping for a quiet holiday with Tyra, just the two of them.

"Do you want to sit for a minute? I can keep the fire going."

"That sounds wonderful."

A strand of dark hair escaped from behind Tyra's ear and brushed her face. She didn't immediately push it away as she would have done when Gordon met her, seven years ago. Her hair was shorter then, cut in sharp angles and streaked with bright purple. She'd come to his shop to deliver a box of kite supplies as a favor to Colleen. Caught in a rainstorm, she had stood in his workroom, dripping and furious, the soggy cardboard box collapsing in her arms. She reminded him of a wet cat, and Gordon was immediately captivated.

Tyra settled into the couch beside him. Folding her legs underneath her, she tucked the blanket around them both.

"Oh wait – I almost forgot." Pushing aside the blanket, she rose from the couch and crossed the room to the hall table. Returning with a letter, she offered it to him. Her eyes snapped with mischief.

"What's this?" The envelope she handed him was plain white, business-sized, hand addressed, stamped. Gordon turned it over. There was nothing on the back and no return address on the front. The postmark, however, was from Portland, where Tyra's sister, Maureen and her family lived. Sliding his thumb under the flap to open it, he removed a sheet of notebook paper, neatly hand printed.

He scanned the words in the first paragraph in utter disbelief. "Is this is about that last game? The one at Thanksgiving? " He read the letter again, this time in disbelief. "I landed on Free Parking and I'm *supposed* to get money for that. Joey was the banker but was texting, so I just took it myself." He let his voice trail off before heaving a great sigh. "We've been over this."

Tyra shrugged. "All I know is that Dilly caught you with a fistful of twenties and your cruise ship was still on 'Electric Company'".

"I rolled an eight. I just hadn't moved yet." Gordon's words were unconvincing, even to himself.

The corners of Tyra's mouth twitched as if she were holding back a smile. "I don't know what to tell you. It sounds like she's got a pretty strong case."

Gordon showed her the page Dilly sent. "Did you see the *title* of this paper?"

"'Code of Conduct.' It looks like she's pretty serious. I guess you two can discuss it when we go over there." This time Tyra did laugh and he smiled in return.

He waved the paper again, so she could understand the gravity of the situation. "I can't let something like this go unchallenged —."

The phone on the end table rang, cutting off Gordon's words.

He frowned. "You can answer this time. I've already spoken to your sister twice. She's given me a list of chores as long as my arm."

Tyra moved toward the phone. "She's just nervous about tomorrow. Maureen put her in charge of shopping this year and I'm not sure she's up for the challenge."

Gordon grunted and turned his attention back to the paper Dilly had sent him, while Tyra answered the phone. "Hello?"

"Hello, Tyra. I'm sorry to be calling so late. This is Arnold Bushwick and I've got a bit of a situation."

The conversation was brief, a quick exchange of information against the background noise of a busy police station. It ended when Tyra offered to make up the guest room for Charlie's nephew.

Tyra replaced the receiver and turned to Gordon, who was still deeply engrossed in Dilly's Code of Conduct. "That was an odd conversation."

Gordon glanced up. "Your sister?" He slid the page back into the envelope. "Okay, if she's that worried about those yams, I'll drive to — "

Tyra shook her head. "It wasn't Lydia. It was Arnold Bushwick at the police station. Charlie's nephew broke into his house – "

Gordon froze. "Is Charlie okay?"

"He wasn't home. Arnold didn't want to arrest Zachary until he could speak with Charlie." She hooked a strand of hair behind her ear. "But this is the part that's strange: Zachary asked for you, specifically."

"Me?"

She nodded. "Said he wanted talk to you if Charlie wasn't home. He said it was important."

Gordon shrugged and pushed the blanket from his lap. "Sure, I'll talk to him. Where is he?"

"Actually, he's coming here. That's why Arnold called — to ask if it was okay. Zachary's got a slight fever." She waved her hand in dismissal. "It's not too bad. Arnold suspects the boy has been sleeping outside. He's having the firemen check him, just to make sure. He probably just needs to rest. Arnold said the station is really busy right now because of the storm, so he thinks Zachary will rest better over here."

Gordon rubbed his forehead with his fingers. "But he broke into Charlie's house. Is he dangerous?"

Tyra shrugged. "Arnold didn't seem to think so, but I can call Arnold back and tell him no if you'd rather Zachary didn't stay here."

Gordon rose from his place on the couch. "No, of course not, Charlie's done a lot for us. His nephew will be fine here for a while." Moving toward the guest room, Gordon snapped on the lights in the hallway. "Zachary's got to be, what, thirteen now?"

Tyra followed him, pulling sheets and extra blankets from the linen closet. "Closer to fourteen, I think. Same age as Dilly." She paused. "He moved away a few years ago." Handing a wool blanket to Gordon, she shut the closet door.

"I think he had just finished third grade the last summer he was here."

Gordon turned toward the guest room, his voice muffled by the pile of blankets he carried. "Do we really need this many? How long is Zachary staying?"

"Just a few hours. Arnold wants a chance to contact his parents and tell them where he is." Snapping open a sheet, she smoothed it across the mattress.

Gordon slipped a pillow into a case. "He's coming over now?"

Tucking the edges in, she laid a down blanket across the top. "Arnold said he needs to fill out some paperwork allowing Zachary to stay here. He's in police custody, technically not under arrest, but they still need a paper trail." Dropping the pillows on the bed, she pushed the corners in. "I think Arnold is trying to spare him an arrest record, especially if the break-in can be straightened out by talking to Charlie."

Gordon folded the wool blanket and placed it on the end of the bed. "He's a teenager." Gordon shrugged. "They can be a bit dramatic."

Tyra waited until Gordon left the guest room before snapping off the light. "Maybe. But doesn't it bother you that we haven't seen this boy in almost five years? Where did he come from? Why is he alone?"

Gordon hooked his arm around Tyra's shoulders as they walked back to the fireplace. "We'll find out soon enough. They're on their way, aren't they?"

Tyra nodded. "That's what he said."

~~~

Hours later, the knock on the door was soft, almost an apology.

As Tyra pushed back the blanket, Gordon woke, rubbing his eyes and blinking. "Is he here?"

"Yes."

Gordon went to the door, welcoming
~~~

Arnold with an open smile and a firm handshake. "Come in — it's cold out there."

As Gordon stepped back to allow them to enter the apartment, Zachary came out of the shadows. The boy Tyra remembered — gentle and tentative, happy to ride bikes and scour the beach for treasures — was gone. In front of her was a slouching teen, head down, hands fisted deep in his pockets. He entered their home slowly, warily, like a predator.

Gordon brushed Zachary's shoulder as he reached to close the door and Zachary started. With a jolt, Tyra recognized the haunted look of a runaway, wary and afraid. She'd seen that look before, many times, in juvenile detention, on kids that had fallen too far into the abyss to be rescued and she hoped Zachary wasn't one of them.

She was younger than Zachary when she was arrested, younger than he was when she went to court, and younger than he was when she was led from the courtroom in shackles and into a van that would deliver her to detention. One mistake made when she was twelve years old destroyed at least three lives, and she'd spent the better part of her own life trying to reverse the damage. Zachary was running from something, something dark, and if he wasn't careful, he'd end up like her.

"Let me show you where you can sleep." Gordon started down the hallway toward the guestroom. As Zachary turned to follow, she watched him.

"I really appreciate this, Tyra. I know it's late." Arnold's voice trailed off.

With a start, she remembered Arnold was behind her. She turned to him. "It's okay, Arnold. He's just not what I expected."

Arnold shifted his weight on his feet. "I know." Arnold's radio crackled to life. "Excuse me, Tyra." He turned away to answer the call.

The door to the guest room opened and Gordon came down the hallway, speaking to them as he approached. "He's settling in."

Arnold turned back toward them, his face apologetic. "I'm sorry, but I have to go. We've got a — "

Gordon stopped him with a quickly raised palm. "It's okay. Go. We can manage here." He opened the door to let Arnold out.

A wave of memories and emotions assaulted her the moment Gordon closed the door, accepting Zachary into their home. The touch on her shoulder made her jump and for a moment she imagined she was back in prison. But it was Gordon. His words were gentle. "It's not the same, Tyra. It's not."

She unclenched her fists and shook off the memory.

~~~

Zachary stood behind the guest room door, listening.

It was stupid of him to get caught in Charlie's house. He'd let his guard down in a moment of weakness and he was dragged from the one place Charlie was sure to go. Holding his breath, he listened at the door but the voices were muffled.

As he reached to open the door, he was stopped by a wave of nausea. It forced him to rest his head on the doorframe and breathe slowly. His breath rattled in his chest and he pushed against the base of his throat to suppress a cough.

Whatever gunk had settled into his chest was clouding his thoughts and slowing him down.
~~~

Maybe they had a pill he could take, some kind of cold medicine. Then he could talk to Charlie with a clear head. The details were important, the circumstances, the money. Charlie needed to know all of it.

When he felt better, he reached for the doorknob, turning it slowly until he could see down the hallway. The cop was still there, talking to Gordon and Tyra. They seemed to be friends, and that was bad. Anything he told Gordon would get back to the cop, and he couldn't risk having cops involved.

It looked like he was on his own.

Again.

Closing the door gently, he moved to the bed and sat. He pulled Charlie's flannel shirt over his head and laid it down on the bed. It was stuffy and hot in this room, but his hands and feet were numb with cold. He tried to swallow past the lump in his throat but couldn't find the spit. And they were still talking outside his room.

Slowly, Zachary closed his eyes. Just until that cop left. Then he could go back outside to wait for Charlie.

Chapter Four

"Tyra, wake up." Gordon's voice was whispered, but urgent.

Tyra snapped awake. The hallway was ablaze with light, and Gordon stood in the doorway, his face ashen . "What is it?"

"Zachary's fever is up — "

"To what?"

"— 104." Gordon crossed the room to pull a sweatshirt from the closet. He threw it over his head, jamming his arms into the sleeves. "I'm taking Zachary to the hospital in Seaside."

"Do you want me to come with you?"

Gordon shook his head and grabbed his keys. "Call Arnold and tell him where we're going. But first, can you help me get Zachary into the car?"

Tyra followed him to the guest room. A twist of blankets and sheets lay across the bed, and the outline of Zachary's dark hair lay stark against the white of his pillowcase. The curtains has been pushed aside, the windows open. Rain spattered against the windowsill and onto the carpet.

"How can I help?"

"I opened the window to cool him down, but it didn't help. Can you bring that blanket, in case — "

"Leave her alone!!" Zachary sat bolt upright, his face a mask of rage directed at something only he could see. "You can't make her do that! She has a record!"

He dropped back onto bed with a sigh and was quiet.

Tyra glanced at Gordon, her hand still clutching the corner of the blanket. "What was that?"

Gordon's face was grim. "The last one was worse." He pulled the blanket from the bed and handed it to Tyra. "I don't know what's going on, but this isn't as simple as a kid running from a restrictive curfew."

"Do you want to try to get his temperature down a little before you drive him all the way to Seaside? What about ice? We can put him in the bathtub and cover him with ice."

Gordon shook his head. "His temperature's been climbing pretty quickly. I'd rather go now. I'm going to drive with the windows down and the air-conditioning — "

"We don't have it! We don't have *any* of it!" Zachary shouted, his voice echoing in the room. After a moment, the fever regained its hold and he sagged against the headboard. "Somebody help."

Gordon's brows creased with concern. "That kid is going through something pretty serious. Too serious for someone his age."

As Gordon lifted Zachary to his feet, Tyra pulled the blanket from the chair and followed him down the hallway. With the passenger seat fully reclined, they buckled him in and wrapped the blanket loosely around him.

"Drive carefully."

Gordon nodded once and was gone.

The moment Gordon pulled away, Tyra punched in the numbers for the Inlet Beach police station. Overhead, the sky had lightened to a pale gray, and the night's rain had turned to mist. It looked like the worst of the storm had passed.

Tyra listened to the phone ring as she climbed the wooden stairs to their apartment.

When Arnold answered, Tyra explained the situation to him as quickly as possible.

He sighed. "I didn't realize he was that sick."

"No one did." Tyra switched the phone to her other ear and pushed the door open. "Arnold, Zachary said some things that lead us to believe he's running from something pretty significant at home. When he's released from the hospital, can he stay with us until we find Charlie? I'd rather he didn't go home until we know if it's safe."

"I'm sorry Tyra." Arnold exhaled. He sounded exhausted. "Everything changed when he went to the hospital. I'm glad Gordon took him — please don't misunderstand — but there are procedures I have to follow now. Child Protective Services will need to be notified."

"Can't you hold off a bit?"

"Why?"

One of Tyra's roommates in detention was a slight blonde girl named Olivia. Almost every night after lights out, Tyra heard the thud of Olivia's shoes hitting the floor and the hiss of Olivia's breath as she drew a blade across the soles of her feet. The night she sliced a tendon, they took her away and Tyra never saw her again. She'd had fourteen placements in fourteen years and none of them lasted more than a few months. Olivia haunted Tyra's dreams, and she wouldn't let the same thing happen to Zachary.

She appealed to Arnold's sense of fairness. "Charlie doesn't even know his nephew is here. And you haven't really had a chance to contact Zachary's parents."

Arnold groaned. "Tyra, I have my hands full with this storm. Clean up tomorrow will be a nightmare. As soon as it gets light, MaryJo will be calling, wanting me to rush final inspections before the Christmas Lights Festival tomorrow night. And sometime, I'm going to need to sleep." He stopped himself and heaved a deep sigh. "CPS has resources that I don't have, Tyra. They'll do what's right."

Tyra's words were rushed "What if I found Charlie for you? What if I found Zachary's parents?"

"I don't think so, Tyra. CPS will take him as soon as I fill out their paperwork and submit it." Arnold's voice trailed off and Tyra held her breath.

"If the doctors at Seaside contact CPS themselves, there's nothing I can do. But I'm busy with emergency calls from the storm and might not be able to file the paperwork until the end of the day."

Tyra exhaled. "Thank you, Arnold. I can find them by then."

"Don't make me regret this, Tyra." Arnold warned.

"I won't, Arnold. Thank you."

Laying her phone on the kitchen table, Tyra slid into a chair to gather her thoughts. It made the most sense to find Zachary's parents first, but he was running from *something*, and it could be them. The haunted look he carried with him did not come from a happy childhood.

Tyra decided to start the search with Charlie, although that might present its own set of challenges.

Charlie had a restless energy this time of year. He had been unusually distracted a few days ago when they anchored the town's Christmas tree in preparation for the storm, so she wasn't surprised that he wasn't home when Zachary broke in. In years past, everyone gave Charlie some space, wishing they could help him and waiting until he came back to himself.

This year she didn't have time to wait.

In the seven years Tyra had known Charlie, she had dialed his phone number so many times that she barely glanced at the numbers anymore, her fingers just knew.

She let it ring six times before she gave up.

By now, Gordon would be at the hospital, and with luck Zachary would have been admitted. Clearly the boy was in trouble and judging by the hallucinations he had last night, it was serious.

A draft brushed Tyra's face and she followed it to the guest bedroom. The window was open and the light beside the bed was lit. A tangle of bedsheets spilled from the bed onto the floor. Tyra reached to pick them up.

Still warm.

She closed her eyes against images of what this boy must be fighting. At his age, his only worry should be math tests and acne. She didn't know what he was running from, so she wasn't sure how to help, or even if she could. What she knew for sure is that her life would have been different if someone had intervened in her life.

After replacing the sheets with fresh ones, she added an extra blanket to the end of the bed. Zachary would need a place to stay when they released him from the hospital, and he would be safe here. Tyra switched off the light and left the room.

She grabbed her cell phone again, this time to call Colleen. She would know where Charlie was. Friends for more than seventy years, Colleen and Charlie met in second grade when she noticed he didn't bring a lunch or dress for the weather. Without asking, she brought him a new winter coat, and until the day Charlie quit school to join the military, she packed enough lunch for them to share. Years later, when Charlie settled back in Inlet Beach, he found Colleen newly widowed and he helped her find her way back into the world. Their friendship was a cornerstone of the community, the closest thing Inlet Beach had to royalty.

Tyra had barely punched in the last number when three shrill beeps blasted from the phone. The recording said that all circuits were busy. She hung up and wondered about driving down to Colleen's house, when a thought occurred to her: a solid fact of life at Inlet Beach was that Charlie never started his day without black coffee from Declan's.

She glanced at the clock. June and Declan might open early to serve volunteers gathered to address the storm damage. If Charlie was anywhere near Inlet Beach, he would be among this morning's volunteers. She would either find him at Declan's or she would be able to leave a message for him.

She had a place to start.

Chapter Five

Pulling her coat from the hall closet, Tyra shrugged it on, adding a scarf, hat, and gloves. Slipping her leather backpack over her shoulder, she opened the door and braced for the cold.

After her release, Tyra had moved to Phoenix, where summer temperatures were hot enough to melt plastic, so the rawness of Pacific Northwest winters still took some getting used to. But she was awestruck by the beauty of Inlet Beach, with fog so thick that it dampened her clothes and left droplets of water on her hair; cedar and pine trees so tall they snagged threads of white clouds right from the sky.

Outside, the air had been scrubbed clean by the storm. The breeze smelled like pine needles, salt, and kelp. The wind from last night's storm had swept away the blanket of gray clouds that hung low in the sky since Thanksgiving. The pink light of the early morning gave Tyra hope for a clear day.

The wooden stairs leading down from their apartment were flecked with ice, and Tyra was careful about staying on the pebbled tread. On the ground level was Gordon's kite shop, Above Your Head, and along the bricked alley were art galleries and gift shops. Even this early in the morning, the shop owners were getting ready for shoppers. Ropes of cedar garland threaded with pinpricks of white light stretched across the storefronts. Planter boxes in every windowsill were filled with evergreens, red berries, and lighted pine cones.

As Tyra walked along the alley to the main street, her boots crunched against the dusting of sand someone had laid over patches of ice. The new art gallery had opened for business already. Its doorway was draped with a string of red stars, and Christmas carols played softly on a radio inside.

More tourists came to Inlet Beach this week than on any other, except for summer.

Families came for the tree lighting and the street fair, with most staying through New Year's Day.

Tyra quickened her step past the office on the end of the alley. That space had been leased to Steven Arshay, the attorney who had handled the inheritance that brought Tyra and her sisters to Inlet Beach seven years ago. She should have filed malpractice charges against him when she had the chance, but it was too late for that now. He'd slithered out of town years ago without a word to anyone.

Further up the main street, people had gathered to repair the storm damage. The worst seemed to be at the intersections, where there was little shelter from ocean gusts. Volunteers collected garbage and righted overturned cans, a few tossed coils of fresh garland from the bed of a pick up to waiting shopkeepers, and others brought tools to repair splintered wooden signs.

It was busy, but no one she asked had seen Charlie, so she continued toward Declan's.

Just down the block, a pair of ladders flanked the sidewalk in front of MaryJo's Dress Shop. Perched on top, MaryJo's husband and son repaired the torn awning, with MaryJo holding the ladder and directing their efforts.

"'Morning, MaryJo. I need to find Charlie, have you seen him?"

Laying one hand on the ladder, Mary Jo brought the other gently to the base of her throat, frowning as she thought. "I don't think so, not this morning." Glancing up the ladder, she shouted to her husband. "Richard! You see Charlie from there?"

Tyra raised her hand to shield her eyes from the morning sun and looked at Richard. Both she and MaryJo waited while Richard scanned the area like a sortie pilot. "Nope," he said, simply, before returning to tack the awning back in place.

"It's important that I find him. If you see him would you ask him to call me?"

"I surely will." MaryJo nodded distractedly as she handed a box of tacks to her husband. When he took the box, she turned back to Tyra. "Have you checked Declan's yet? Seems likely he would be there."

"I'm going there now." Tyra eyed the damage to the storefront. In addition to the torn awning, one of the shutters had blown loose and the plastic reindeer that had stood in front of her shop for years were missing altogether. MaryJo and her family would be outside for quite a while. "Can I bring you something? I can ask June to make you up a thermos."

MaryJo smiled. "Thank you, but Richard's almost finished up there. We'll be along in a minute or two."

It didn't look to her like Richard was anywhere near finished, but Tyra thanked them both, and left.

Hunching her shoulders against the gusts from the ocean, Tyra turned and crossed the last street, but her pace slowed when she saw the crowd in front of Declan's. It overflowed the front door and spilled onto the sidewalk. Her heart pounded in her chest. Years spent in confinement wasn't something easily overcome, and a fear of enclosed spaces was one of the scars that remained.

With a deep breath to steady her nerves, she shouldered past a tangle of sleepy tourists. Inside the shop, a Glenn Miller version of "Sleigh Ride" played on speakers mounted in the corners of the room. The sound, blended with the yeasty smell of warm cinnamon scones and the rich aroma of freshly pulled espresso shots, worked its magic, and she felt her body lighten.

Scanning the crowd, Tyra looked for Charlie.

He *should* have been seated in his usual spot by the gas fireplace, sipping his coffee and holding court. Instead, his chair was occupied by a smug little hipster with a pony tail and wire-rimmed glasses. A trail of crumbs scattered from the empty plate in front of him, spilling onto the floor. With his legs crossed at the knee and his attention riveted on the screen of his tablet, he was oblivious to the crowd of people waiting for a place to sit.

As she turned to leave, someone called her name. It was June, Declan's wife and co-owner of the shop. Her thick dark hair was swept into a pony tail and her cheeks dimpled as she smiled. Tossing a bar towel over her shoulder, she gestured to an empty seat at the end of the counter.

"What do you think of this year's entry?" June pulled the hem of her sweater away from her body so Tyra could see the whole pattern.

Tyra groaned. June's sweater was possibly the ugliest thing Tyra had ever seen. The collar and cuffs were outlined with multi-colored flashing lights. A tree made entirely of gold tinsel adored the front and the hem was laced with jingle bells. Tiny Christmas stockings plastered both arms.

Tyra rolled her eyes. "You're going to win this year, June. I've never seen anything that bad."

June flapped her hand in dismissal. "Oh it's not finished. I still have more to add. I plan to take the title back from Gordon this year."

Tyra dropped her pack onto the seat of the chair, not intending to stay long. "Well, I wish you luck. Do you know who's judging this year?"

June shook her head with a scowl. "I can't believe no one will tell me."

A bell jingled as the front door opened. A group of women erupted in laughter and squeals as they entered, and Tyra turned to look. "You said you would die before you put a bell over the door."

June paused, a cardboard drink tray in her hand. She glared at the door. "Declan said it would be nice for Christmas. He put it up without telling me."

Dropping three paper cups into the tray slots, she filled them with coffee and added lids. "Can I get you something?" She pointed to the sad assortment of coffee mugs on the shelf behind her, and her eyes twinkled. "I bet Gordon wouldn't mind if you used his mug."

Almost as long-standing as the Ugly Christmas Sweater contest was the tradition for residents to leave a personal coffee mug on the shelf at Declan's. Over the years, it had become a bit of a competition to display the ugliest. So far, Gordon was the clear winner with something he created in a winter ceramics class at the community center. Lumpy and thick, the handle was crooked, the base sagged, and the color was an uneven mash of drips and spots.

Tyra shook her head. She would never use that mug. Gordon probably used house paint to win the contest. Now that she thought about it, she'd never seen anyone drink from that mug.

"No, thanks. I'm fine." She glanced at the crowded shop before turning her attention back to June. "I didn't expect you to be so busy. I'm looking for Charlie, and it's kind of important. Have you seen him?"

June had been filling a paper bag with pastries from behind the counter. She paused and cocked her head. "Arnold is looking for Charlie, too. He called early this morning and told me what happened last night." She looked away and her voice trailed off. "I can't believe that boy's back." Cutting herself off with a quick shake of her head, she folded the bag closed and set it next to the drinks. "Anyway — Arnold asked us to keep an eye out for Charlie and to call him over if he came in." Her eyes widened, as if something had just occurred to her. "Did Charlie drive to Seattle again?" She let out a long breath. "Colleen's going to kill him this time."

Tyra hadn't considered Seattle.

Just after Thanksgiving last year, Charlie had disappeared for over a week. He had been restless then, too, before he left. He mentioned something vague about wanting to investigate a restaurant's claim that it had the best coconut cream pie in the Pacific Northwest. Without telling anyone where he was going, he drove up the coast to Seattle and stayed almost a week. He found a hotel by the market and spent his time wandering, chatting with the merchants and watching the vendors throw fish.

Colleen had been frantic.

After three days of not knowing where her friend was, she called the State Patrol in Oregon and in Washington, explaining that an elderly man with a heart condition was missing. She begged them to look for him. Eventually, they brought him home to Inlet Beach, sputtering and indignant. It took every bit of Arnold's professional influence to smooth things over when the police discovered that Charlie did not, in fact, have a heart condition nor was he lost.

Tyra cupped her face with her hands and groaned. "He wouldn't have done that again."

"Let's hope not. They didn't speak to each other for almost a week." June's gaze swept the entire length of the shop. "I had to burn sage in this place when it was all over."

A gust of wind blew in the open front door, rustling papers behind the counter. June glanced up, her brow furrowing, then changing to a smile when she saw who it was. Tyra turned as

June raised her hand and called out. "Billy — over here."

Billy navigated the crowd from the front door to the back of the shop, pulling a red wool scarf from his neck as he went. Technically a volunteer, he had been deputized by Arnold as a junior cadet as soon as he entered middle school. He received a special badge, and was allowed to run errands on the weekends and after school when his mother let him.

As he moved closer, he squinted behind wire rimmed glasses as they fogged in the warm air of the shop. Tyra moved the chair so he wouldn't trip.

"Hi, Billy. You're out early this morning." June reached for Billy's mug from the shelf. The patrolmen from the station donated it as a welcome present when Billy joined the force. It was white, with a blue Inlet Beach insignia, the only mug that looked safe to drink from.

Billy nodded, beaming. "Arnold's working a case, and Jerry came over from Seaside to help us with storm damage." With a crooked smile, he straightened his posture, pushing his shoulders back ever so slightly. "Arnold *himself* called me in. Said the department needed my help coordinating things because everything has to be inspected before the Festival tomorrow night."

June filled the mug with hot chocolate.

After adding a squirt of whipped cream, she offered him a folded paper napkin and a smile of encouragement. "That's good news, Billy. He must really depend on you."

Billy's cheeks pinked and he raised the mug to his lips to hide his smile.

June added a chocolate muffin to the bag and placed it beside the carrier. There are three of you at the station now? You and Arnold and Jerry?"

Billy pulled the mug from his mouth, eager to answer. A splash of hot chocolate sloshed over the side and onto the counter. He swiped at it with his napkin. "They're doing more than just storm inspections." He leaned over the counter and whispered. "They have a case." His eyes widened, and he corrected himself. "I'm not listening to conversations, that wouldn't be right. And I can't tell you anything officially because it's an on-going investigation. "

June placed a fresh napkin next to Billy's mug. "Of course. Don't tell us anything if you can't."

As Billy looked away, his expression clouded with disappointment. He liked being on the force, liked when people asked him questions. After a moment, he took a deep breath, apparently finding a loophole. "I suppose if we're going to solve the case, we're going to need help, so I'll tell you some things." He raised his index finger to clarify. "*Some* things. Not everything; I can't tell you everything. They are looking for the family of a boy named Zachary Wallofski. Arnold found an old address for him in Ashton."

Ashton was an old logging town fifty miles from Inlet Beach, not connected to anything by a major road. No busses. No train. Zachary was too young to drive. So how did he get to Inlet Beach?

Billy leaned into the counter and lowered his voice "He didn't have much luck there. When I came in this morning, the Ashton police called back to say she wasn't there, and that the neighbors think she left town." Billy shook his head. "The address before that was a trailer out by the processing plant but that's old. She never paid rent and when the police went to evict her, she'd already gone. Left the landlord with a mess." He frowned in disapproval. "He was not happy about that."

"That's a lot to find out in such a short time."

Billy nodded sagely. "Arnold's the best."

Billy unzipped his jacked and pulled out a nylon wallet from an inside pocket. As he peeled back the Velcro, June shook her head. "This is on the house, Billy."

"But they told me I could use the department credit card." Billy furrowed his brows.

June smiled. "And think of how happy they'll be that you are saving them money."

Billy didn't seem to understand so June added. "You are all working so hard over there– with the storm and the investigation — that I'd like to give you this as a 'thank you'".

He brightened. "Like a present?"

"Exactly like a present."

"Okay. Thank you."

As he turned to leave, Tyra slipped her backpack over her shoulder. "I need to get going too. If you see Charlie, will you call me?"

Tyra paused. June knew everyone at Inlet Beach, and most of their secrets. "Why do you think Zachary needed to see Charlie so badly?"

June sighed. "I honestly don't know."

"You don't think he wanted to hurt Charlie, do you?"

June's brows furrowed. "He never seemed like that kind of kid to me."

"I'm surprised Charlie doesn't talk about him more. I know he's awfully old to be Zachary's uncle, but they seemed so close. I was surprised when Zachary moved away and we never heard from him again."

"— uncle?" June tilted her head. "Tyra, Charlie is not that boy's real uncle. His relation to Zachary's mother is only by marriage, and even that's being generous. Charlie hasn't seen that boy in years, not because he didn't want to but because he hasn't been *allowed* to."

"What?" Tyra felt a chill touch her spine but shook it off.

June's eyes narrowed with disgust.

"Tiffany — Zachary's mother — forbade Zachary to come to Inlet Beach or to ever talk to

Charlie again. Two summers is all she allowed them."

"Why?"

"I don't know. Charlie won't talk about it."

"Colleen?"

"She's never said a word."

"Does Arnold know this? "

June shook her head. "I don't see why he would."

"June? We're out of change." The cashier's voice was whispered, her eyes wide. The line of customers waiting for caffeine reached to the door, many of them with crossed arms and raised eyebrows.

"Coming." Her cheeks reddened as she laid her hand on Tyra's arm. "Tyra, I'm not completely sure that what I said is true. It was just something I heard the summer Zachary didn't come back. I probably should have kept it to myself."

June hurried off and Tyra sank to the chair. Why was she wasting her time looking for Charlie if he wasn't a relative?

~~~

From deep inside Tyra's leather backpack came the sounds of "Macho Man" by the Village People, the ringtone Gordon assigned himself and downloaded onto her phone one day when he was bored.

When Tyra answered, the connection crackled, and the background noise of the hospital chopped his words. Pressing the phone against one ear, she plugged the other with her finger, hoping to hear him better.

"Can you say that again? I didn't hear you."

"It's good news, Tyra. The x-ray confirmed pneumonia, but it's not severe. The complications are from exhaustion and dehydration. They've already given him a shot of antibiotics for the pneumonia and he's on an IV drip for fluids."

"That's really good news, Gordon."

"It's going to take most of the day to get him stable enough for discharge. I thought I'd stay with him."
~~~

"Will they let you bring him back here when they release him?"

"I hope so. He's not under arrest. But the social worker has been giving me stink-eye all morning. I don't think she likes me."

"Try to avoid her, if you can because —"

A loudspeaker page at the hospital cut off her words. As she waited for the announcement to end, the phone crackled with static. She spoke louder, hoping Gordon could hear but she couldn't be sure he did.

When the announcement ended, Gordon returned to the phone and his words were rushed. "I have to go, Tyra. The social worker is coming this way. She doesn't look pleased —"

"— Gordon, wait."

But Gordon had already hung up.

~~~

Tyra took a deep breath and exhaled slowly. A small complication, but no need to panic. If Charlie wasn't Zachary's real uncle, there was still plenty of time to contact Zachary's parents. Ashton was a tiny town less than an hour's drive
~~~

away, and she had more than eight hours before Arnold had said he had to file paperwork with CPS.

She just couldn't shake the feeling that sending Zachary back to what he ran away from was a mistake.

Then an idea sparked: Colleen.

Colleen knew every secret at Inlet Beach. She would know if Tyra was wasting time looking for Charlie. She probably knew about his parents. Colleen would know what to do.

Lifting her backpack onto her shoulder, Tyra waved to June and left the shop.

The walk from Declan's to the Animal Hospital where Colleen worked was mercifully short. As she was leaving Declan's, a stray gust of wind from the ocean across the street pulled the door from Tyra's fingers and banged it against the building. And although the sky had cleared, the effects of the storm lingered offshore. Ocean waves rolled and crashed, churning spray as they crested. Blasts of wind pulled the spray from the ocean and spit it across the beach. Pulling her collar to her ears, Tyra hurried toward the Animal Hospital where Colleen worked.

The building was sheltered from the ocean, and as she approached, the wind stilled. Standing outside the door, Tyra unbuttoned her coat, shaking the mist from it. As she turned to enter, Tyra spied the decorations at the entrance, and she grinned.

Every Christmas, despite guidelines from the Merchants Association, Colleen decorated as her mood dictated. Last year, a field of plastic reindeer and elves lit the entrance. Arnold had pleaded with her to clear a path through the sidewalk, so Colleen convinced Charlie to mount the reindeer on the roof. The elves stayed where they were.

This year, apparently, she had been inspired by blue. The roof line dripped with dancing blue icicle lights and blue snowflakes as big as manhole covers hung in the window. In the window boxes, evergreens were laced with blue and silver ribbon and dusted with glitter. Tyra's smile widened. She knew for a fact that MaryJo, as head of the Merchants Association, had specified a single rope of tasteful white lights outlining every building, with a drape of garland across the storefront.

Inside, the lobby of the Animal Hospital was warm and smelled like cinnamon, pine cones and beeswax. Too early yet for patients, Colleen sat behind the reception desk, shouldering the phone against her ear, deep in conversation. Glancing up when Tyra entered, Colleen indicated she was almost finished. With her emerald-green reading glasses firmly in place, she recited an order from a pink sheet of paper.

She shifted position in her chair. The air around her crackled with annoyance, though her smile remained firmly in place. "Well, Henry, of course we appreciate you coming all the way out here. Next time, we surely will get our order to you sooner." A pause. "Yes, I understand that

Inlet Beach is out of your way." Widening her smile, Colleen said. "Well, you have a good day, too."

Heaving a sigh of resignation, Colleen plunked the receiver onto the phone cradle and shuddered. "Hateful man."

Tyra snorted back a laugh. "Who is?"

Colleen looked up from the page, scowling. "The drug rep. He doesn't think we order enough for him to make the trip out here but once a month."

"Have you placed an order with them yet? Because ever since Mulligan was a patient, you've only ever asked for samples."

Colleen waved her hand in dismissal, not even bothering to answer the question. Then, stuffing the page into her desk, she swiveled her chair and gestured to the seat beside her.

Tyra draped her coat on a nearby chair and sat. Colleen removed her glasses and set them on the desktop. "If I remember correctly, and I do, you don't appreciate the early hours of the morning. So what gets you out of bed so early, and over to see me?"

Tyra shifted in her seat. She should have given this more thought. Telling Colleen that Charlie was missing would upset her. Telling her that someone had broken into Charlie's house would be worse.

Colleen tilted her head, the hint of a smile crossing her lips. "Oh, honey, I am not nearly as fragile as you might think. He went to Seattle again, something about gingerbread this time."

"He's not answering his cell phone."

Colleen rose from her chair to switch on the tea kettle. After pulling two mugs from the cabinet, she turned. "He probably forgot his charger. Technology is not a friend to that man." She tapped a box of peppermint tea. "How about some tea?

Tyra bit back a smile. They'd had this conversation before, many times. "I'd love some. Green please."

Colleen grimaced, but pulled out a tea bag from a box she kept only for Tyra.

"Do you know what hotel he's staying in?" Tyra tried to keep her voice casual, but Colleen turned, her eyes deepening with concern.

"Of course I do. Why?"

"Last night his nephew Zachary came to find Charlie. He broke a window in Charlie's house and Arnold took him into custody until he can locate either Charlie or Zachary's parents. Because he can't find either, Arnold is required to notify CPS. I am concerned that CPS will return him to his parents or remove him altogether and that won't address what he's running from."

The tea kettle whistled in the background.

Colleen paled, her fingers still resting on the box of tea. Her voice was jagged. "Seeing that boy again will break Charlie's heart."

Pulling her chair out, she sat down and sighed. "My mother was right: a secret will always make its way into the light."

"Is Charlie Zachary's uncle? Should I be looking for Zachary's parents instead?"

She glanced up, eyes sharp. "Zachary only knows his mother, Tiffany. She's loosely related to Charlie, but by marriage only." She paused, her fingers clasped so tightly together that the knuckles were white. "That's an important distinction because things would have been a whole lot different for that child if Charlie was a blood relative."

Peeling the plastic from a plate of sugar cookies, she slid the plate toward Tyra. "Tiffany was fifteen when she had Zachary. From the beginning, he was left alone earlier than he should have been, and for longer than was right. When Charlie found out, he went over to visit because he thought all she needed was guidance and she could be a good mother."

Colleen paused, closing her eyes. "The stories he would tell me when he returned from her trailer would break your heart."

Clasping her hands and gently rubbing her thumbs, she continued. "When it came time for him to enter kindergarten, he didn't go. I wanted Charlie to call CPS right then, but he wouldn't."

Looking down, Colleen traced the chain of her eyeglasses with her index finger. "And when he didn't go to first grade either, I called CPS myself. Without telling Charlie."

"They investigated. Tiffany said she homeschooled the boy." She scoffed. Pulling a napkin toward her, she rolled the edges between her fingers. "That girl is not nearly smart enough to homeschool."

"The next year, they put him in second grade but he struggled. He didn't know how to do anything the other kids had already learned: couldn't spell his name, didn't know his address, and couldn't count past ten."

A piece of the napkin tore free. "That was the first summer Zachary stayed with Charlie. He taught Zachary to read. Took him to the dentist for his first check up. By September, he was ready for third grade. New clothes, new shoes, and a satchel filled with school things."

"So what went wrong?"

"This is quite a conversation, isn't it?" Pushing her chair back, Colleen rose and hurried to the tea kettle. Touching the metal with her fingers, she frowned. "I'm afraid it's gone cold." Lifting the lid, she peered inside. "I'll just add some fresh water. Won't take a minute."

Tyra's words were rushed, her voice sharper than she intended. "We don't have time for this." Taking a breath, she continued. "I'm sorry, Colleen, but if Tiffany is still as bad as you say, and Charlie's not a relative, then CPS is going to take Zachary. What kind of home do you think they'll be able to find for an angry teenage boy? I have seen the result of bad placements and I won't let it happen to Zachary. You need to tell me everything. Please."

Outside, a little girl in a bright red coat ran by the window, on her way to the beach. Someone called to her and she turned, laughing, and waited. Her father ran to her, scooped her into his arms and hoisted her to his shoulders.

Together they crossed the street to the beach stairs.

"You're right." Colleen returned the kettle to its base, and moved slowly toward her desk. "You have a chance to do what Charlie and I failed to do six years ago." When she spoke again, her face had paled and her voiced was ragged. "We let that little boy down, Tyra. We did. And I don't know why we thought that was okay."

Tyra reached across the desk for Colleen's hand. "Why did the summer visits stop? We never saw Zachary after the second summer. We thought he'd moved away."

Reaching for the napkin, Colleen smoothed a crease as she answered. "Tiffany wanted money." She drew a deep breath. "She saw Zachary's new school things and I guess she wanted a part of that for herself. All that next year, she'd call Charlie for money, saying it was for school. It would be easier, she said, if Charlie just sent the money and she would buy the things herself." The napkin shredded under her fingers and Colleen pushed it away. "One day, about a week before school let out for the summer,

Tiffany called and said that if Charlie didn't pay her for Zachary's company, she wouldn't let him come. So Charlie paid."

"How much?"

"Twelve hundred dollars."

Tyra didn't realize she had gasped until she heard the sound echo in the room.

Colleen brushed the corner of her eye with a fingertip. "You've seen how Charlie lives, bless his heart. The kindest, most generous man I know, but he's never had a head for business. He chooses his projects because they interest him and for no other reason. Somehow he found the money that year and paid her."

Her smile was watery. "That summer was the happiest I've ever seen him. Charlie and the boy were inseparable. Zachary had his own little tool set and a place at Charlie's workbench."

"Zachary didn't come back after that. What happened?"

Colleen looked away. In the distance, a space heater switched on, the hum echoing in the still room. "It was me. I am the reason Zachary was forbidden to see Charlie. I knew she would want more money and I knew Charlie didn't have it so I drove over to try and reason with Tiffany."

Colleen snorted. "Nothing I could say would change her mind and that was the last time Zachary was allowed at Inlet Beach. Charlie was so worried that he made an appointment to see that attorney, Steven — do you remember him? The attorney who handled the beach house for you and your sisters."

Tyra shifted in her seat. Of course she remembered that man. Grossly incompetent, Steven Arshay knew nothing about family law, but his greed would have compelled him to take the case and pretend to be an expert. Any advice he offered Charlie would have been worthless.

Colleen looked away. "Steven researched the case but in the end was sure that Charlie didn't have a chance at permanent custody. So Charlie let the matter drop."

"And that's why he let everyone think Zachary moved away."

Colleen nodded. "It broke his heart."

"Do you have any idea why Zachary would want to find Charlie after all this time?"

"I don't know." Colleen's voice trailed off, and Tyra waited. The fan on her computer clicked to life, and, when she spoke again, her words were soft. "We should have done more to help that little boy."

Tyra glanced at the clock and rose from her chair.

Colleen glanced up. "Where are you going?"

Shrugging on her coat, Tyra answered. "It seems I've been looking for the wrong person. I need to find Tiffany."

A storm of emotions swirled in her chest. Anger against Steven who would have billed Charlie for a case he didn't research. Disbelief that Colleen would have valued Charlie's feelings over Zachary's welfare. And, the most powerful: rage against Tiffany, for renting her son to a man who loved him. But Tyra tamped them all down because she needed a clear head if she was going to help Zachary.

Chapter Six

Gordon signed the last form and handed the clipboard back to the social worker. "Is that it, then?"

The woman pursed her lips as she flipped the pages and when she reached the last one she snapped them back in place, nodding curtly. "We have a perfectly adequate recovery room at the Center —"

"— where he will be handcuffed to the bed."

"— where his condition will be monitored until he is processed. I shouldn't have to remind you that the boy is in police custody." Having made her point, the woman's lips thinned into a white line.

"They haven't filed charges, and you don't know if they will. The words came out sharper than he intended. Gordon drew a breath and steadied his voice. "He's fourteen, so, technically, right now, he's just a sick kid who needs a doctor."

This woman was too quick to label Zachary, and Gordon refused to let him become a checkbox on her day's worksheet.

The social worker turned to the nurse's station and leaned over the counter, catching the eye of a nurse working at a computer. "What is Zachary Wallofski's progress? Room 2187."

Although the nurse's smile appeared accommodating, her expression was haggard, as if she'd already put in a full day and still had hours left before she went home. After tapping a few keys on her keyboard, she glanced up from her screen. "The IV is the last thing in the doctor's notes." Sliding a clipboard from a stack, she trailed the page with her finger. "But the doctor wants to check him before he's released. She flicked her gaze to the social worker. "Or moved."

"Thank you." Gordon offered his best smile, but she had already returned to her work.

Snapping her pen behind the metal clip, the social worker trapped the board against her chest. "I need to check with my supervisor. These rules are in place for a reason. I'll be back shortly."

Gordon nodded, his head pounding from lack of sleep. He wouldn't let Zachary be moved but if she talked to her supervisor, they might discover that Gordon was just Zachary's ride to the hospital and that his opinion didn't matter.

He made his way to the surgical waiting room, the only place he'd found with good cell phone reception. A dark little cave littered with stained chairs, battered end tables, and arrangements of ugly plastic flowers, the room smelled strongly of antiseptic. A mounted television blared from the corner, and the laugh track grated his nerves. Reaching up, he snapped it off before sinking into a hard plastic chair.

Pulling his cell phone from his shirt pocket, Gordon scrolled to Tyra's number. With luck, she'd already found Charlie and everything could be straightened out before lunchtime.

Tyra's cell phone rolled immediately to voice mail. After leaving a brief message, he rose from his chair and walked to Zachary's room to await the social worker's decision.

~~~

As his bagel traveled the rickety conveyor, Charlie eyed the block of cream cheese in the bowl in front of him. Dumped into a plastic bowl and forgotten, ice shards floated in a puddle of milky water and flecks of toast lay scattered across the top. When the bagel clunked down the chute, edges blackened and smoking, Charlie's heart sank.

A woman squeezed ahead of him in line. Snatching a bruised apple from the fruit basket, she held it with grubby fingers and offered him a weak smile. "You didn't want this last apple, didja?"

Charlie didn't. He didn't want any of it. Not his bagel. Not this hotel. Not the long drive home. His body ached from a restless night in an unfamiliar bed and a dull headache throbbed from behind one eye. He wanted his own bed, a good sleep, and strong coffee from Declan's when he woke up. He was getting too old for this nonsense.

He managed a polite smile. "You go ahead."
~~~

She jabbed a dirty finger toward his bagel. "Dont'cha want anything on that?" She pointed to the floating cream cheese and a crusty jar of grape jelly. "The jelly and all's over there."

Turning, she shouted toward a table filled with children. "You kids need anything while I'm up? Make sure you all take something for lunch. We're not stopping."

Because she was blocking the coffee pot, Charlie waited as she folded a stack of stale pastries into a wad of paper napkins. When she returned to her table, Charlie filled a short cup with burnt coffee.

A man in a dull green uniform wheeled a trolley to the buffet. He wiped the table with a grimy white rag, pushing the crumbs onto the floor. Digging a handful of teabags from a box, he stuffed them into the wire basket and wheeled the trolley away.

Charlie took his coffee and dry bagel back to his plastic chair in the lobby to watch the weather reports.

The desk clerk smiled at him as he passed. "It shouldn't be too much longer, Mr. Gimball.

They said the highway to Seaside has just been cleared."

Charlie managed a smile. "Thank you, but I'm headed to Inlet Beach."

"Oh."

~~~

Balancing a deli bag containing three boxed lunches and a tray of drinks, Tyra entered the tiny police station of Inlet Beach. She slid them across the reception desk, next to the scrubby plastic Christmas tree and a bowl of wrapped mini-candy canes. The room smelled like stale donuts and burnt coffee.

Arnold looked up from his desk. His eyes were bleary and his face was shadowed with stubble. "Hey, Tyra."

"What are you still doing here, Arnold?"

Dropping his pen on the desk, Arnold pushed back his chair and stretched. "I'm headed home now. Things have calmed down since this morning, although we're still short-handed.

Jerry's been called back to Seaside."

"Billy's gone, too?"
~~~

Arnold nodded. "His mother said he had to finish his science project before the Christmas Lights Festival tomorrow."

Tyra pulled a boxed lunch from the bag. "I brought lunch for you guys. Take this one even though you're leaving. You can eat it on the way home."

Arnold offered a weary smile. "That would be great, thanks." As he pushed his chair back from the desk, something caught his attention and he paused. When he looked at Tyra, his smile was grim. "You should probably know that the social worker at the hospital has asked to take Zachary to the recovery center as soon as his last IV is complete."

"Can she do that?"

Arnold shook his head. "Not without my permission. But if they look into this any closer, they'll wonder why I haven't filed paperwork on a minor in protective custody. Time is running out, Tyra. I'm supposed to have all my paperwork filed before my shift ends. And my shift ended —"

Arnold flipped his wrist to consult his watch.

"— nine hours ago."

"What if we found Zachary's mother? Then you won't have to notify CPS at all."

He rubbed his palm over his face. "The latest address took four hours of phone calls and dead ends. The police in Ashton said the area was an old logging area, an illegal squatter's camp now. They sent a patrol car but she wasn't there and the neighbors weren't helpful."

Tyra pulled a drink can from the tray, topped it with a plastic straw and slid the whole thing toward him. "So what happens now?"

"Honestly, Tyra? I'm done. I need to get a couple of hours of sleep because I still have inspections before the festival." He scooped his lunch and grabbed his coat. "It might not be such a bad idea to pull in CPS on this. They'll investigate and they won't send him back to live where it's not safe. He'll be taken care of."

A whisper of an idea presented itself to Tyra but if she asked Arnold's permission, he would have said no. So she didn't. Instead, she held the door for him. "You've done all you can. Thank you Arnold."

Arnold turned to leave, raising his hand to wave as he stumbled to his car.

After Arnold pulled away, Tyra removed the second lunch box and found Carl in the break room, eyeing a stale donut. She handed him a lunch. "Here's something better."

Carl dropped the donut in the box. It landed with a thud. "Thanks Tyra."

She waited until he took a bite, then asked very casually. "Arnold said he'd found an address for Zachary's mother, Tiffany. Do you happen to know where he put it? I can't seem to find it."

Carl swallowed and nodded. "Yeah, on his desk. Yellow legal pad near the phone." Cracking open his drink can, he brought it to his lips and drank.

On her way out, Tyra pulled out her phone and took a picture of the address. Then she called her sister.

She had one lunch left and she hoped it would work as well on Lydia as it did on Carl.

Chapter Seven

Tossing her backpack and the last boxed lunch into the passenger seat, Tyra settled into her car and turned the key. While the defroster melted the frost still lacing the windows, Tyra pulled out her phone and called her sister.

Lydia answered on the second ring, her voice frazzled. "Tyra, is Gordon with you? Has he found those yams for Maureen yet?"

After switching on her Bluetooth, Tyra pulled her car onto the main road. "Lydia, I need a favor."

"Can it wait? Maureen's coming tomorrow and I haven't done anything on her list."

"You've never cared about Maureen's lists before. Why now?"

Lydia was silent for a moment. When she spoke again, her voice dripped with guilt. "I may have used the grill plate."

"What?"

Lydia's reply was soft, almost a whisper. "On the stove."

The stove in the beach house was Maureen's prized possession and a bone of contention among the sisters. With two ovens, six gas burners, and a grill plate down the middle, Maureen's stove cost more than Tyra's first car. When they rebuilt the beach house, Charlie and his crew cut a hole in the sheetrock just to allow them to bring the stove into the house. It was enormous and Maureen loved it, and she didn't like anyone to use the stove without.

Tyra was incredulous. Maureen would have Lydia's head on a platter if anything happened to that stove. "Did you break it?"

Lydia's reply was immediate, but dripping with guilt. "Of course not." Her swallow was audible. "I may have scratched the grill plate a little — trying to clean it — but the scratches aren't really noticeable."

Tyra saw her opportunity and exploited it as only a sister would. "If I help you clean the stove, will you do me a favor?"

Lydia's voice was wary. "What kind of favor?"

"It's a long story but I need help finding someone." Tyra slipped her car into neutral as she paused briefly at the last stop sign in town.

"What information do you have and how recent is it?"

Tyra smiled. Lydia loved solving puzzles. The rest would be easy.

Shifting into first gear, Tyra continued through town. "I have an address in Ashton but the neighbors told the police she'd left town."

Lydia scoffed. "Of course they did. Nobody talks to the police."

Tyra pushed the clutch, downshifting as her jeep climbed the hill.

Lydia sighed through the phone. "Okay. " Lydia took a breath. "You don't have a lot of information, so what you need to do –"

Tyra's tires crunched on the driveway as she approached the house.

"Wait is that you — did you just drive up?" The white eyelet curtains moved as Lydia looked out the kitchen window.

"I need you to come with me."

"Come with you?" The curtains fluttered as Lydia snapped them shut. "Forget it. Maureen is coming tomorrow. She expects me to have the shopping done and I haven't even started. I don't have time to come with you."

Tyra waved the deli bag. "I brought you lunch."

"Ashton is a hundred miles from here."

"Fifty." Tyra corrected, and then she brought out her best offer. "If you come, I'll clean the entire stove myself and I'll take the blame if Maureen notices anything. That will give you time to shop for food."

Lydia's response was immediate. "Deal." Then she amended: "But you have to swear, and then we are never to speak of this again. You can never — ever — use this against me. No matter what."

"Done." Tyra agreed. "Bring your laptop and your cell phone. You're going to need the internet. You should bring your portable printer, too."

Lydia sighed. "I'll bring my whole bag."

As Tyra waited, she mapped out a strategy. If Zachary was running from his mother, she could be dangerous. It wasn't fair to bring her sister into a situation like this without telling her everything.

As Lydia opened the car door and slid into the passenger. As she buckled her seat belt, she said. "Maureen is my favorite sister, you know. She would never do this to me."

Taking her hand off the gear shift, Tyra shifted in her seat and faced her sister. The choice to come had to be Lydia's, with full knowledge of what might await them. "Do you remember little Zachary? The boy who spent two summers with Charlie during the time we restored the beach house? He broke into Charlie's house last night."

Lydia opened her mouth to speak but Tyra shook her head. "Charlie wasn't home. It's a long story but Zachary's in the hospital now, with pneumonia. Unless we find a relative, CPS will take him into custody. An old address for his mother is all I've got, and I don't know what we'll find when we get there." A strand of hair brushed her cheek and Tyra impatiently hooked it behind her ear. "What I *do* know is that a regular foster home is not a good choice for an angry teenaged boy."

Lydia blinked. "Wow. No wonder Gordon's not answering his phone."

"I'm serious, Lydia. I can't bring you to a place that is potentially dangerous without you knowing everything going in."

Lydia nodded and unhooked her safety belt. "Lemme change my shoes."

When she returned to the car, she was dressed completely in black, head to toe. She looked like a ninja and Tyra rolled her eyes.

Lydia snapped her seatbelt, looked at Tyra. "What?"

Tyra pointed to the glovebox. "You're going to need the internet. Charger's in there."

Tyra pulled out of the driveway and onto the main street. She drove toward Tiffany's last known address, wondering what they'd find, and hoping she wasn't making a mistake.

~~~

The GPS had given up forty minutes ago and had left breadcrumbs for the last fifteen, so at the very least they could find their way back to the main road. Lydia stabbed the screen with her finger. "We have been down this way at least three times. There isn't anything here."

"The guy at the gas station told us that the address was this way."

"This is a logging road, there's nothing here but sadness." Lydia pointed to a muddied path dug into the side of a hill, frozen and shadowed by enormous pine trees. "Wait — are those tire tracks?"

Tyra slowed the car and flicked on her headlights. It had been drizzling rain off and on for the better part of the afternoon, and weather conditions made the drive longer than it should have been. The pale winter sun had given up and was fading into an early twilight. Soon it would be impossible to see anything, especially on a wooded road with no street lights.
~~~

Switching her Jeep into four wheel drive, she said, "We might as well look."

The path turned out to be frozen mud, easier for traction, but the unfamiliar area demanded concentration. Neither of them spoke as Tyra drove down the narrow road into the woods. Lydia gripped the handle above the door, her expression grim.

"It's got to be down this road, Lydia. There is nothing else around here."

Lydia didn't respond, and one glance in her direction explained why. The berm on her sister's side had dropped about twenty feet, creating a deep ravine. Unless they found a place to turn around, Tyra would need to travel this same road, this time in reverse. And it would be fully dark by then. Tyra tightened her grip on the steering wheel, and they drove in silence as the woods around them melted into shadow.

Lydia pointed to a break in the trees. "I think that might be something — over there."

In the clearing, a collection of rusted trailers and campers circled a muddied field. Tyra pointed to a wooden shack, about the size of a tollbooth, behind a pile of twisted lawn chairs and garbage. Cracked sheets of plywood covered the windows. Beside it, the skeleton of a battered cargo van rested on cement blocks, long threads of blackberry vine entwining its frame.

Lydia's voice was almost a whisper. "This can't be right."

"There's nothing else around." Tyra pointed to a board scrawled with numbers, nailed to the front door. "Five-something-something-seven. The address we're looking for is five-two-one-seven."

They sat for a moment in the car, its headlights slicing into the twilight.

Lydia spoke first. "I can't believe you brought me here."

"I can't believe Zachary *lives* here."

"And what we're doing is important?"

Tyra nodded. "It really is."

Lydia thought for a moment. "Does anyone know we're here?"

"Just Colleen."

"Terrific." Lydia's eyes narrowed as she glanced around the settlement. "That one." She pointed to a rusted trailer near the front of the compound. A blue light flickered behind a dingy window covered with a torn bedsheet. "That one has electricity. Let's go."

They walked through the field to the trailer, past broken boards, rusted beer cans, and jagged glass bottles. With each step, Tyra wished she had the wrong address. No one should be forced to live here.

The mist changed to drizzle as they climbed the stairs to the front door, and Tyra zipped her coat to her neck to keep out the chill. From the top of the stairs, she glanced again at the logging shack. The utility lines had been cut and lay snaked and forgotten on the ground. Thick blackberry vines reaching across the weeds had claimed it, covering the wire almost completely.

Lydia's knocks were answered with a yipping dog and a slurred voice commanding it to shut up.

The same voice called through the door. "What do you want?"

"We're friends of Zachary."

"So what?"

The chill she had been trying to avoid settled into Tyra's bones as she realized that what

Zachary was running from could very well be this woman. She reached for Lydia's arm to pull her back.

Lydia shook off Tyra's grip and raised her voice. "Have you seen him?"

The door opened a few inches, though the chain remained firmly in place. "He lives in the back." The woman pushed her arthritic finger past the chain and pointed to the abandoned shack behind the trailers.

Tyra stepped in front, ignoring her sister's glare. "He's not there. Have you seen Tiffany? It's important we find her."

The woman narrowed her eyes. "She ain't here." Stepping inside, she closed the door and drew the chain.

Lydia touched the closed door with her fingertips. "Charlie Gimball sent us."

Behind the door was silence. After a moment, the woman replied, speaking through the door. "How do you know Charlie Gimball?"

"We're from Inlet Beach. Zachary went to see Charlie."

The chain unbolted and the door opened, revealing an older woman, a halo of tight pincurls helmeting her doughy face. A ratty fleece blanket wrapped her body and she gripped a shivering little dog in the crook of her arm.

"So he made it, did he?" Her eyes narrowed, her gaze sharpening.

Lydia nodded. "He did. But we have to talk to Tiffany. It's important."

The woman shook her head. "Won't do you no good."

She tried again. "Zachary's sick. He's been taken to the hospital."

"When he left, he only had a cold." The woman's gaze darted between Tyra and her sister. After a moment, the woman nodded sharply. "Go wait in your car. She'll be along directly."

Lydia practically bounced down the stairs. "That was easier than I thought it would be."

The mist had turned to rain again, making the walk to the car cold and wet. A breeze rolling off the hill pushed the weather toward them. Shivering, Tyra dug her hands deeper into her coat pockets and ducked her head. While she admired her sister's optimism, she was quickly losing hope.

Inside the car, Lydia pulled her laptop from the back seat and switched it on.

"What are you doing?"

"I have an idea."

"Do you need help?"

"Nope." Her sister's eyes were bright with excitement. "I've got it."

Tyra turned to look out the fogging window, hoping her sister's plan would save them. Lydia's track record for this kind of thing was excellent, but Tyra kicked herself for coming here without any sort of plan. Did she think that a brief conversation in a squatter's camp would make everything okay? Tyra came only because a kid needed help. But what she really did was ensure Zachary's delivery to CPS, driving him further from Charlie.

Lydia's portable printer whirred to life just as Tyra heard the trailer door slam.

"That must be her." Tyra pointed to a painfully thin woman descending the stairs, one hand gripping the railing and the other holding a black garbage bag. A lumpy green coat encased her body, its hood pulled over her head, hiding her face.

Slipping the printed sheet into a folder, Lydia opened the car door and slipped out.

Tyra and Lydia crossed the field and met her at the bottom of the stairs.

With nicotine-stained fingers, the woman pushed the matted, fur-trimmed hood from her face. Greasy hair was gathered into an elastic and lay limp behind her ear. Scowling, she looked up, her eyes unfocused, the irises constricting to pin points.

"So he ran to Charlie, did he?" Dropping the bag to the ground, she brought her fingers to her neck and scratched. Her nails left a trail of angry red welts but she appeared not to notice. "I told him Charlie didn't want him. So what do *you* want?"

Tyra felt anger growing in her chest but she pushed it down. Anger wouldn't help here. "Zachary is sick. He has pneumonia and he's in the hospital at Seaside."

Tiffany shrugged and lit a cigarette. Her fingers trembled. "He shouldn't a runned."

She tried again. "The hospital will only release him to a relative —."

Tiffany's laugh cut her off, a sharp bark that revealed several black teeth. "I show up and they stick me with the bill. Nice try, though." She picked a fleck of tobacco from her coated tongue.

"What about Zachary?" Lydia sounded incredulous.

"He made his choice." Tiffany sniffed and wiped her nose with the back of her hand. "Inez told me to talk to you and that's all I'm doing. I need to leave here and I got a ride coming. We're going someplace warm."

Drawing the printout from her folder and a pen from her pocket, Lydia stepped forward. "Let us take care of Zachary while you're gone. He'll be warm and well fed. We can enroll him in school if you're not back by the time the new term starts."

Tiffany spit on the ground. "Why should his life be any easier than mine? I was knocked up at his age, left to fend for myself. Nobody took care of me."

Charlie tried, Tyra wanted to say. *You should have let him. Things would be different if you had.*

In the distance, the rattle of a loose muffler drew closer as a battered pick-up truck rumbled down the narrow road toward them.

Drawing a final drag from her cigarette, Tiffany flicked the stub into the brambles. "This is my ride." Reaching for the plastic tie of the garbage bag, Tiffany started to lift it from the ground.

Tyra stepped in front of her. "Let me tell you what Zachary's life will be like if you leave without signing that paper." Her heart pounded as she thought of what awaited him. "Child Protective Services will take custody of your son when he's released from the hospital. If he's lucky, the social workers will try to place him in a good home, but that placement won't last because he won't let it. So they'll try another and another and another. But in four years Zachary will be eighteen and they won't be able to help him. What will he do then? Where do you think he'll go?"

An image of Olivia's last letter flashed before her. Her placement didn't work, she said, but she had been promised another. This time it would be a family, with sister and brothers, she said. She'd finally have the older sisters she wanted. Tyra never heard from her again. The rumor was that she took her own life.

Lydia continued the thought, her voice rising as the truck approached. "After they take your son from you, they'll want to know how he ended up that way. They'll want to talk to you, Tiffany. How close to your life do you want CPS to be? How closely do you want them to look?"

The truck pulled up in a cloud of blue smoke, angry music thumping through the open window. The driver turned the music down and shouted out the window. "Get your skinny butt over here or I'm leaving!"

Tiffany ignored him. She looked up, her eyes flat and defeated. "I didn't mean it to turn out this way."

The driver punched the steering wheel. The horn blast bounced against the hills and disappeared into the trees.

"Charming." Lydia muttered.

Tiffany's glance cut to Lydia and she shrugged. "He wasn't my first choice." She turned and shouted to him. "Hang on a second" He responded by turning the music up and lighting a cigarette. "You have about a minute until he starts getting antsy."

Absently, Tiffany pushed up her sleeve to scratch a rash on her arm. Silver threads of scar tissue crossed the veins of her wrist. Letting her sleeve drop, she turned to the driver.

Lydia offered the paper to Tiffany again. "Sign this paper and you can go."

Tiffany glanced from the paper to Tyra. Her eyes narrowed, her voice was edgy and mean. "And what do I get?"

Lydia blinked. "Visitation, Tiffany. You can visit him — "

Tyra cut her off, matching Tiffany's low voice with a growl of her own. The discussion about a boy's future had become a prison yard exchange and it was revolting. "What do you want, Tiffany?"

"Well," Tiffany glanced at the waiting driver. They watched as he flicked his cigarette butt out the window. "I don't want to go with him."

"Okay."

"I need money and a ticket outta here."

"Done."

Tiffany smirked. Turning to the driver, she hardened her expression. "Gw'on! I changed my mind, I ain't going."

The driver swore and slammed his truck into gear. Mud and rocks spun from his tires and he left in a cloud of smoke.

Tiffany turned to Tyra, her expression unchanged. "You better not be playing me."

"We're not your enemy, Tiffany. We're here to help."

"Help Zachary, you mean. You wouldn't be here if it wasn't for him."

"You have more options than he does." Tyra countered.

Tiffany bit her lip. "How much money you got?"

Both sisters spoke at once: "A hundred." "Fifty-six."

Tiffany narrowed her eyes. "I chased him away for a hundred and fifty-six dollars?" She snorted. "Tell ya what: "I'll take the cash and Charlie can have Zachary for Christmas, but that's all."

Lydia sneezed. Pulling the collar of her coat tighter against her neck, she sniffed. "Listen.

It's getting late and I'm cold. Here's what's going to happen. We will give you all the cash we have. We will drive you to a bus station and buy you a bus ticket to wherever you want to go." She leveled a look of her own. "But this offer ends as soon as we get into the car. You have one minute to decide."

Tiffany stared at the page for so long that Tyra wondered if she could read. "We will take care of him, Tiffany. You get a fresh start away from here."

With an almost imperceptible nod, Tiffany took Lydia's pen and scrawled her name at the bottom of the page. As Lydia folded the paper and slid it into her bag, Tyra watcher Tiffany for any sign of maternal instinct. Any sign of regret that she wouldn't be the one to care for her son, but she saw nothing.

When Tiffany looked up, her eyes filled with greed. She had already forgotten her son. "Anywhere I want?"

Tyra concealed her disgust. "Yes, Tiffany. Anywhere."

~~~

Charlie lifted the paper cup from the middle console, sipped, and immediately regretted it. Bitter and thin, no matter how much cream he added, it couldn't come close to what they served at Declan's. At least drinking it kept him occupied on the long drive back to Inlet Beach. With a grimace, he dropped the cup back into the holder. Too late for coffee anyway, even if it was decaf.

Ten miles outside of Inlet Beach, the road narrowed from two lanes to one. As the setting sun dipped behind the trees on his left, long shadows appeared across the highway, and Charlie switched on his headlights.

He was almost home now.

A spatter of rain from the trees overhead hit his windshield, startling him. Cracking the window and turning on the radio, Charlie hoped the radio's company and fresh air would clear his head.

Approaching the exit for Inlet Beach, he flicked his turn signal and slowed. Fastened to the base of the exit sign was a sandwich board for the
~~~

Community Theatre advertising its production of *A Christmas Carol.* Charlie had helped build some of the sets and he wished them well, but he wouldn't attend the performances.

Charlie envied Ebenezer Scrooge. The Ghost of Christmas Past visited Ebenezer only once. Charlie's own Ghost was relentless, arriving every year just after Thanksgiving and staying through New Year's. The memories it brought were jagged and sharp. The Ghost drew him into the past and abandoned him there to relive drunken fights, rage, and beatings, and it suffocated him. So when Charlie left town unexpectedly, it was only because his Ghost had forced him to run.

Again.

Pausing at the bottom of the Inlet Beach exit, Charlie considered his choices. A left turn at the stop sign would take him through town, to hot coffee at Declan's and maybe a visit with Colleen. He could check on the town's Christmas tree in the square. A right turn would lead him home, undetected, though side streets. Home to a hot shower, a warm meal, and his own bed.

He turned right.

After easing his truck into the garage and switching off the engine, Charlie propped his elbows on the steering wheel and scrubbed his face with his hands. He had been running from Christmas for as long as he could remember, and he was exhausted. He understood some people waited all year for this holiday, decorating their homes and yards, singing carols, baking cookies.

But Charlie wasn't one of them.

Gathering cups and papers from the cab of his truck, he walked down the driveway to the trash cans to throw it all away. In the dim light of late afternoon, Charlie crossed the front yard, surveying the damage from the wind storm. It was mostly fallen branches and a dusting of pine needles, nothing that needed his immediate attention. Without the energy to go around the house, he climbed the front steps and unlocked the door, intending to go straight to bed.

Chapter Eight

Tyra climbed the wooden steps from the alley to her apartment, her head buzzing from driving too much and from lack of sleep. She wondered how to tell Gordon that they might have custody of a fourteen-year-old boy, and how to tell Zachary that his mother left him.

After trudging to the top of the stairs, she blinked. Mounted on the front door was a softly lit wreath, tied with a wide gold ribbon and dotted with glittery red balls. Because she and Gordon spent Christmases with her family at the beach house across town, they never bothered to decorate their apartment. She didn't think they even owned decorations.

Slipping the key into the lock, she opened the door. Inside the air smelled of warm garlic bread and spicy chili simmering on the stovetop.

In the corner of their apartment near the tall windows was a tree, fully decorated and dripping with threads of silver tinsel. The table, usually a dumping place for newspapers, mail, and project notes, had been cleared and spread with a bright red cloth. In the center was a basket of evergreen branches and cinnamon-scented pinecones.

From the kitchen came a soft thread of Christmas music playing on the radio and the sound of a pot lid clattering against a pot, sounds not usually heard in her house. Tossing her keys in the basket and stuffing her coat in the closet, she went to investigate.

Appearing extraordinarily pleased with himself, Gordon stood before the stove wearing a green apron outlined in red garland and printed with flying reindeer. The kitchen was clean, bread was warming in the oven and a giant pot of chili simmered on the stove.

Tyra stood in the doorway, absolutely stunned. "Did you *cook*?"

Gordon waved his wooden spoon in dismissal. "Of course not. Marjorie sent rosemary bread over from the bakery — cinnamon rolls too, for tomorrow. Declan made the chili." With his wooden spoon, he gestured toward a box lying on the countertop. "We've got Christmas cookies, Tyra — *lots* of them."

"When did you have time to decorate? Or pick up dinner? How long have you been home? Did Zachary help? Is he here?" Tyra peppered him with questions.

Gordon shook his head, his blue eyes twinkled. "You don't understand. All of this, — " He swept the spoon across the entire, decorated apartment. " — was here when we got back — the decorations, the dinner, everything. Colleen did it. She left us a note saying that Zachary needed a memorable Christmas, and a fresh start."

Gordon pulled Tyra close to him, and she melted against his chest. As she listened to his heartbeat, the coils of stress across her shoulders began to loosen. As she exhaled, a thought occurred to her. "How does Colleen have a key to our apartment?"

His chest rumbled with laughter. "She left us *cookies*, Tyra. I don't care how she got a key. I hope she uses the key on Easter, too."

The beginning notes of "I'll Be Home for Christmas" played on the radio and, with a jolt, Tyra remembered Zachary.

Pushing away, she looked at Gordon. "Is Zachary here? CPS didn't take him, did they?"

"Nope. He's here. He's been sleeping since we got back from the hospital and he appears to be much better. I was just about to wake him up for dinner."

As Gordon started for the door, Tyra pushed her hand against his chest to stop him. "Wait a minute! How did you get CPS to let you have Zachary? You're not a relative."

Gordon shrugged. "I may not be a relative but I *am* an official Inlet Beach Deputy now. Zachary is still in protective custody and I was authorized to transport him back. Arnold himself faxed the papers to the hospital. He said it would give you more time." Picking up the spoon to give the chili a final stir, he looked at Tyra. "Did you find Tiffany?"

"Colleen told you?"

Nodding, Gordon laid the spoon down and turned off the stove. He reached into the cabinet for bowls. "She called me after she talked to you.

She called Arnold too, to tell us both where you were headed." He turned to frown. "I wish you hadn't gone out there alone. Colleen didn't paint a generous picture of Zachary's mother."

Tyra opened a drawer and pulled out soup spoons. "I didn't go alone, Lydia went with me."

"Good for her. She's tougher than she looks, your sister." Gordon stacked three plates on top of the bowls. "How bad was it?"

With Zachary safely asleep, Tyra told Gordon the whole story. What Tiffany looked like, where she was going, and who she intended to go with. That Tiffany had the look of an addict, and that she was worried Tiffany might be into something more than that. Then she showed him the paper and waited for him to read it.

Gordon leaned against the counter to read the paper, his expression grim. "So that's it, then? She's gone?"

Tyra nodded.

"Do you know where she went?"

Tyra shook her head. "Lydia and I drove her to the bus station in Astoria and bought her a ticket for San Diego. But we didn't see her get on the bus. Tiffany could have cashed the ticket in."

She sighed. "She could be anywhere and I couldn't stop her. She refused to come to Inlet Beach, even to see her son."

~~~

Zachary woke with a start. Blinking in the unfamiliar room, he assembled the pieces of the last two days, his confusion lifting. After rubbing his eyes with the heel of his palm, he pushed himself upright and took a tentative breath. The antibiotic shots he didn't want may have been a good idea after all. The tightness in his chest had lifted and his headache had calmed to a dull pounding.

His stomach growled. Pulling a sweatshirt over his head, he slipped his feet into dry sneakers, eager to see the decorations and hoping he wasn't too late for dinner.

Not letting Gordon help him had been a mistake, one he would fix, now that he could think more clearly. Gordon stayed with him while the nurses took care of him, waiting in the chair even when he pretended to be asleep.

Zachary opened the door to the sound of voices, at first too muffled to be understood. Slip-
~~~

ping from the room, he moved through the hallway to the kitchen and listened.

Gordon spoke first, his voice deep and rumbly. After a brief hesitation, Tyra answered, her voice softer and harder to understand. He moved closer, to just outside the kitchen, catching snippets of the conversation, words that made the blood pound in his ears.

"....... bus station in Astoria ... ticket for San Diego.....she could have cashed the ticket in......could be anywhere....wouldn't come to Inlet Beach, even to see her son."

The words peppered him like a spray of bullets. His vision tunneled and the room stilled. He heard himself speak, the words loud in his ears, louder than he intended. "What ticket?

Tyra and Gordon whirled around to face Zachary, their eyes wide. But they didn't answer, so he clenched his hands and screamed.

"WHAT TICKET?"

What happened next seemed like a dream, where everything moves in slow motion. He saw them come closer, Gordon's frown, Tyra reaching for him. He saw their mouths move but all he could hear was a scream echoing in his head.

He struggled to sort everything he'd heard, but none of it made sense. Their explanations dissolved in the air and disappeared like smoke.

His mother was gone. She left and he wasn't enough to stop her. She knew he was at Inlet Beach and she wouldn't come.

Chapter Nine

Zachary ran.

He slipped down the stairs and through the alley, clawing branches of evergreen from window boxes as he went. His chest heaved and his vision blurred, and still he ran. He ran until he stumbled, collapsing into a heap on the ground.

Falling back against the wet grass, Zachary gulped for air. His heart pounded in his ears. Pulling deep breaths into his lungs, he waited for the world to make sense again. Gradually, his pulse slowed, and feeling returned to his arms and legs. His face cooled as he felt a light mist falling on his skin.

Across the square, a bell jingled as a shop door opened and a group of people emerged. Their laughter echoed in the still night, fading into the darkness as they walked away.

"Look at the tree, Mommy! Look at the tree!" A little girl wearing a puffy blue coat jumped with excitement in front of the Christmas tree in the town square. The branches dripped with a million white lights, the glow blurred in the falling mist.

Zachary watched the mother move closer, taking the girl's small hand in her own as she pointed to ornaments on the tree. The father joined them. With a growl, he scooped the child into his arms and she squealed with joy. As the family walked away, the mother leaned toward the father as he draped his arm around her. The three shadows merged into one and it felt like a punch in Zachary's gut.

His fingers clawed the grass, curling around a jagged rock, squeezing it in his fist, liking the solidness of it and the feel of the edges slicing into his palm.

He'd never had that, never had a family. He didn't know his father, and he was almost ten years old before his mother bought a Christmas tree. It came from the liquor store, with mangled branches and reeking of stale gin.

Drawing back his arm, Zachary hurled the rock at the tree but it disappeared into the branches. Scrabbling for another rock, he rose to his knees and threw that one as hard as he could. But the branches swallowed that one too.

With a howl of rage, he advanced on the tree. Clawing the branches, he hooked a string of lights and ripped them away. Grinding them under his heel, watching them explode against the sidewalk. With both hands, he pulled a branch until he heard it give way with a satisfying crack. As a line of glass balls slid down the broken branch, he smashed them into the street and hurled them against the shops across the street, imagining each ornament as a grenade. His heart pounded and his arms trembled, but he didn't care. He hated Christmas.

"Hey!"

Zachary froze. The destruction he caused was everywhere. The street and sidewalk was littered with tangled strings of broken lights, jagged glass ornaments, and splintered tree branches.

He didn't mean to do this, didn't want to destroy the tree. He turned, and ran again.

~~~

The chime of the doorbell pulled Charlie from a dream and he woke to darkness. He had intended only a short nap, but it appeared he had slept through both dinner and the evening news. His nerves snapped with irritation. If that was Colleen at the door, come to lecture him about being away again, he'd have a thing or two to say this time.

Charlie rose from his bed, slipped on his bathrobe and pushed his feet into his slippers. Drawing the flannel against his shoulder, he pulled the belt ties tight just as he reached the front door. Flicking on the porch light, he unlocked the door, ready to defend his right to leave town whenever he wanted.

"Hi, Charlie."

"Tyra?" Charlie squinted against the light of the porch. "Why are you here so late? Is everything okay?"

"No, Charlie, it's not okay right now, but it will be. We need your help. Can I come in to explain?"
~~~

As Charlie stepped aside to let Tyra in, he peppered her with questions. "Is Colleen alright? You and your sisters? Gordon — "

Tyra laid her hand on his arm. "We're all fine. Can we sit down? I have a lot to tell you."

"Kitchen. Let's go to the kitchen." Charlie led the way, flipping the light switches as he went.

A square of cardboard taped to the window caught his eye, strange because of the location. Too obscure to be wind damage, the cardboard wasn't there when he left. He'd have to figure that out later.

Pulling a chair from the table, he waited until Tyra was seated. "What is it, Tyra?"

Tyra shook her head, her expression urgent. "Could you sit down please?"

Charlie sat.

She pointed to the damaged window. "That damage was caused by a break-in. It was Zachary, Charlie. Zachary Wallofski ran away from home and came to Inlet Beach to find you."

Charlie slumped against the back of his chair. As Tyra explained, a chill crept into the marrow of his bones and settled there. He heard nothing beyond the idea that Zachary came to find him. And that was all he needed.

Pushing his chair back, he stood. Reaching for his coat and slipped it over his bathrobe. "Let's go."

Chapter Ten

As Tyra drove through town, Charlie's thoughts spiraled. What would bring Zachary to him after five years? Was he in trouble? Was he hurt? Did Tiffany know her son was here? The questions formed so quickly that he couldn't put a voice to them, so they drove in silence until they came to the edge of town.

"Charlie, I know this is a shock but there's more."

In the space of three blocks, she told him so much that Charlie staggered under the weight of it all. Had that boy really walked all the way from Ashton to Inlet Beach? Turning his head, Charlie looked out the rain-spattered window into the dark night. Zachary would have slept outside in weather like this.

When they got to the edge of town, Tyra parked near the beach stairs, behind a patrol car. Arnold stood beside it and Charlie fumbled for the door latch and rushed toward the car. "Is Zachary under arrest?"

Arnold shook his head, his face shadowed. "Not yet. I'd rather keep this between us for as long as we can. The damage to the Christmas tree is pretty significant. If I get complaints, I'm going to have to take action."

"Where is he?"

Arnold pointed to the beach. "Gordon found him under the beach stairs." Arnold offered Charlie a blanket. "He's probably cold. You're going to want this."

"Thanks, Arnold. For everything." The blanket smelled like lavender. Charlie thought of Colleen and wished she was there because she would know how to make everything all right. Charlie had no idea where to start. It had been so long.

Holding firmly to the railing, Charlie shuffled down the stairs in his slippers. As he descended, the light became dim, and Charlie wished he'd brought a flashlight. Tucking the blanket under his arm, he continued, slowing his pace, unsure of his steps. When the wood gave way to sand, Charlie sank to his knees and crawled behind the stairs.

"Uncle Charlie?" The voice was deeper than Charlie expected. Hoarse and whispered, as if Zachary couldn't believe Charlie was real.

"I'm here." Charlie reached into the darkness.

"Uncle Charlie." The words were a sigh, as if Zachary had just laid down a heavy burden and could rest. He came into the dim light, melted into Charlie's arms and began to cry. "I'm sorry. I'm so sorry."

Charlie listened as Zachary cried, remembering the boy as he held together the fragments of the teen he'd become. As the sobs turned to shudders, then faded to hiccups, still Charlie held tight. Only when the boy had quieted, did Charlie finally speak. "They told me what happened. Are you alright?"

When he felt Zachary's nod, he released the boy and shifted his weight in the sand. "Come over here with me. Let's sit down."

Spreading the blanket across the bottom step, Charlie made room for Zachary to join him. Then he waited for the boy he hadn't seen in five years.

As Zachary emerged from under the stairs, Charlie stifled a gasp. In his heart, Zachary was still nine years old, pudgy-faced, with wide front teeth and an open smile. The teen before him was lanky and pale; his movements controlled and quiet, as if he didn't want to call attention to himself. When Zachary sat down, the light shifted and Charlie noticed the hollows in his cheeks and the tightness around his mouth, and he winced.

He could have prevented this.

If he had sold his truck or his house or his land it might have kept the boy safely in Inlet Beach for years. Another lawyer might have found a way to secure custody and Charlie blamed himself for not trying hard enough.

He took Zachary's hand. It was icy and covered with bruises. His palms were lined with scrapes and patches of dried blood. For the first time, Zachary looked up and met Charlie's gaze. In his eyes was a torment that a boy his age should never have to endure.

Charlie cupped Zachary's hands in his own, hoping to warm them. But he couldn't find the right words to take away Zachary's pain. A quick glance to the street above showed Gordon had joined Arnold and Tyra, all of them watching from a distance. Tyra was better at this than he was, better with people. He wished she would come down.

Zachary shifted on the blanket, and Charlie felt him shiver. Unbuttoning his coat, Charlie slipped it over the boy's shoulders and tucked it around his neck. Maybe he was getting sicker. The thought caught in Charlie's throat. "Do you need to go back to the hospital?"

Zachary shook his head.

"Does your mother know where you are?"

He felt Zachary shrug, and Charlie cringed. It was a stupid question. Drawing a breath, he tried again. "Okay, then. Why did you come?"

Zachary slipped his hands from under Charlie's, folded his arms over his chest and stared toward the ocean. "Mom's boyfriend. He's a bad guy."

Charlie's heart skipped. "Did he hurt you?"

Zachary shook his head. "He moved in. Gave us money so Mom quit her job." He mouth twisted with disgust. "Right after she quit, he demanded the money back. All at once."

"But your mother didn't have it because she'd quit her job."

Zachary scowled. "And she wouldn't look for another one."

In the distance, the surf crashed and the night air chilled as a mist rolled in from the ocean. Charlie stifled a shiver, tucking the collar of his bathrobe around his neck, and he stayed where he was.

Zachary shifted his weight on the step and continued. "He said she didn't have to work if she didn't want to. He liked where we lived, said it was isolated, and no one would bother him." Zachary turned, his eyes blazing. "She's already been in jail, Uncle Charlie. The judge warned her— "

"— warned her? Jail?" Charlie struggled to keep up. "When was she arrested? Why didn't anyone call me? Who took care of you when she was in jail?" He sputtered questions as soon as they occurred to him but he stopped cold when he felt Zachary shrink from him.

Charlie spoke immediately. "I'm sorry."

The boy nodded. "It's okay."

"No, Zachary. I mean, for everything. I knew what your mother was like. Even when you were little and spent those summers with me, I knew what she was like. I should never have sent you back to her in September. I should have found a way to keep you safe. I didn't, and I'm afraid I've let you down." Charlie laid his hand on the boy's shoulder and Zachary leaned in. Encouraged, Charlie continued. "I'd like you to consider living with me. "

Zachary opened his mouth to speak, but Charlie rushed his words. "— only if you want to. Gordon and Tyra want you to stay with them, of course. But I'd hoped —" Charlie cleared his throat. "I'd like you to — I've missed you."

"What about my mother? Tyra made her leave town."

Charlie shook his head. "That's not the way Tyra explained it to me."

Although it broke his heart to do so, Charlie repeated most of what Tyra had told him about her conversation with Tiffany, leaving out parts he hoped Zachary would never find out. "Your mother knows where to find you, and she might surprise you one day with a visit." Charlie shook his head, not wanting the boy to live years on a thread of hope. "But in the meantime, we'll make a home for ourselves, right here. I'll see about getting you back into school after Christmas, and we'll figure the rest out as it comes up."

There was one more thing to address, and Charlie didn't want to do it. The boy had suffered enough, but Charlie needed to start as he meant to finish. "The Christmas tree in the square."

Zachary nodded as he looked away.

"I don't believe you meant to, but you damaged something that means a lot to the people who live here and the families who come to visit. I'd like to know why you did it."

Charlie glanced at Zachary but couldn't read his expression. Maybe it would be better if Charlie fixed the tree himself. The boy had been though so much already.

Zachary's voice cracked. "It was because of the family."

After a long moment, Zachary spoke again. His voice was flat as if he were narrating a movie. "They were looking at the decorations together. The mother was holding her hand."

Zachary bit his lip, his face hardened. "I was eight years old before I learned Christmas trees are supposed to be inside your house, decorated. With presents."

Zachary hesitated, and Charlie waited for him to continue. "I must have bugged her about getting a tree of our own too often, because one day she pulled a scrubby plastic tree from a liquor store bag. She was really angry." Zachary looked at his hands. "She stuffed the base of the tree into a coffee mug. Told me to decorate *that*, told me to 'knock myself out'. Then she locked herself in the bedroom. Two days later, she staggered out, drunk and smelling like stale gin and vomit."

Zachary snorted. "Christmas was over."

Zachary turned to look at Charlie, his eyes filled with pain. Charlie drew Zachary closer and said the first thing he could think of. "I don't like Christmas either. It's hard to be a part of a celebration when your own memories are so different. But if you destroy decorations because it hurts you to look at them, you're stealing a chance for someone else to make a good memory.

Zachary's brow furrowed and Charlie rushed to make his point, wishing he could find the right words. "That little girl might remember that tree and holding her mother's hand for the rest of her life. Destroying the tree would have taken that from her."

Charlie let his voice trail off, embarrassed to be so philosophical. Abruptly, Charlie pushed himself to his feet. "We'll figure everything out in the morning. Right now, we need to get some sleep. I'd like you to go back with Tyra and Gordon."

"They won't want me after what I've done."

Charlie pointed to the road above the beach stairs. "They've been up there waiting, the whole time we've been talking. Gordon is the one who found you, and Tyra came to get me. They're good people, Zachary."

After Zachary rose from the stair, Charlie brushed the sand from the blanket. "You've got a bed there already. We can deal with the tree in the morning; it's too dark to see anything now. If we get there early enough, no one will notice until we fix it."

Zachary hesitated. "Uncle Charlie?"

"Yes?"

"Thank you."

Charlie smiled as he put his arm around Zachary and guided him up the stairs.

Chapter Eleven

Zachary refused to sleep. Shifting and turning under the blankets of his bed, he kept himself awake. There was one thing left to do, and Zachary wanted to be the one to do it, so he waited. When the sky lightened to gray, then melted into pink, he pushed away the covers and got dressed.

The door creaked as it opened, and the floorboards groaned as he crept across the room. Zachary winced at every sound. In the kitchen, he opened cabinets and drawers until he found garbage bags and a pen. After scribbled a quick note on the back of an envelope, he escaped into the early morning.

The bricks in the alley were slick with ice, and Zachary navigated carefully to the street. He retraced his steps from the night before, his breath clouding in the chill of the morning. When he arrived at the town square, he pulled one of the garbage bags from his backpack and got to work.

By the time the pink sky had deepened to purple, Zachary had gathered the last shards of glass and tied the last garbage bag. After dragging it to the curb with the others, he assessed his work. He had restrung lights that seemed undamaged but he couldn't be sure without testing them. He'd redistributed the remaining plastic ornaments on the tree, but there weren't enough, and the branches he'd cracked created a hole in the tree big enough to walk though.

Snatching his backpack from the grass, he headed for the ocean to think. Years ago, he used to spend hours wandering the beach with his friend Dilly. Together, they had built sandcastles and villages, decorating everything with driftwood flags and sea grass forests. He wondered where Dilly was, and if she would remember him.

As he approached the surf, the wind whipped in from the ocean, carrying sea spray with it. The beach was still deserted but tourists would be waking soon, and when they came to town, they would notice the tree. Digging his hands into his pockets, Zachary wished he could surprise them, and Charlie, with a newly-decorated tree. He didn't want to ask anyone for help, but he couldn't see a solution.

Before he realized it, he had walked the entire length of the beach, from beach stairs to the state park. The last house on the beach was the one Tyra and her sisters inherited the first year he came to visit Charlie. The switchback trail up the hill and into the yard was before him, covered with sea grass sprinkled with winter frost.

The summers he lived at Inlet Beach with Charlie and played on the beach with Dilly were some of the best memories of his life. Dilly had had a bright yellow beach bag that they collected everything in, and the sand dune they had raided was just ahead. In the summer the dune was scattered with flowering shrubs and seagrass. This time of year, the seagrass faded to a silvery gray and all that remained on the bushes were white and red berries.

Zachary stopped in his tracks, goose bumps rising on his arms.

That was it.

That was the solution.

Pulling the hem of his shirt away from his body, he gathered sea grass and berries, driftwood and pebbles, mussel shells and sand dollars, and piled them into the pouch of his shirt.

~~~

Maureen stood at the top of the trail leading from her house to the beach, sipping the last of her coffee. Always the first in her family awake, she was about to start her favorite part of the day: her early morning walk on the beach.

When she saw Zachary scurrying around the shore like a sandpiper, she watched. And when she realized what he was doing, she smiled and returned to the house to wake her family.

~~~

The sea grass snagged his fingers as he braided, but Zachary didn't stop, tucking the berries into the strands as he went. In the corner of Gordon's workshop, a space heater clicked on, and the sound echoed in the still room. He rubbed his hands together; the heat would be welcome.

Nine braids of sea grass lay lined up before him on the table. He planned to join the ends and make wreaths, a job that would be easier if he allowed himself to use glue. A pot of kite glue sat on a shelf not four feet from where Zachary sat, but he didn't have permission and he wouldn't steal.

Zachary pushed his shoulders back to stretch his muscles, ignoring the bubble of panic forming in his chest. Nine wreaths of seagrass wouldn't be nearly enough to cover even the barest parts of the tree. The damage was sure to be noticed by now. Ignoring the growls from his stomach, he rushed his work.

He had four wreaths completed when he heard the voices approaching the workshop. Zachary froze, remembering when he broke into Charlie's house and set off a silent alarm. If Gordon's workshop had an alarm, and he triggered it, he would surely be arrested this time.

The window he had jimmied to enter was directly behind him. If he left immediately, dropping his work on the table and abandoning everything, he could escape undetected. No one could prove he was there.

Or.

He could wait, explain what he was doing, and ask to be allowed to finish the decorations.

He chose the option that would make Charlie proud.

~~~

The first one through the workroom door was Dilly. Taller and older, her face was slimmer but her eyes were still the same. They danced with laughter and Zachary felt himself smiling in return.

Crossing the room quickly, she dumped a yellow canvas bag onto the wooden table and heaved a sigh. "Do you have any idea how *cold* it is out there?" Shedding her coat, she tossed it to a chair and claimed the stool next to him, eyeing the pitiful stack of wreaths he'd made. "Why aren't you using glue?"

Zachary opened his mouth, but didn't know what to say first. The words swirled in his head and he couldn't find the right one.

Gordon came through the door next and Zachary steeled himself for the rebuke he knew would come. He was in Gordon's workroom with-
~~~

out permission, and as he watched Gordon approach the workbench, Zachary dropped his gaze.

Gordon deposited a stack of driftwood in the center of the table. "Glue would make that job easier."

"I didn't — "Zachary's voice caught and he cleared he throat. "I didn't want to use your stuff unless you said it was okay."

Gordon paused for a moment, then nodded once. "Good decision." He moved to a bank of storage shelves, removing and distributing glue pots, nylon kite thread, and twine. After claiming a place at the table, he glanced at Zachary and winked. "Help yourself."

Zachary felt his shoulders relax.

The door clattered open again. Dilly's older brother, Joey and her older sister, Juliette entered, windblown and pink-cheeked. Setting their buckets on the table, they let the door slam behind them.

It banged open again a moment later.

Dilly's father entered, juggling a tin bucket in one arm and a clutch of grocery bags in the other. Dropping everything on the table, he nodded a greeting to everyone at the table as he unwound the scarf from his neck.

Gordon peered inside the bucket to examine the contents and his laughter, deep and booming, echoed in the room. He pointed to Joe's bucket. "*That's* what you bring?"

Joe turned, scarf in hand and shrugged wearily. "I just do what I'm told."

Zachary sneaked a look at the contents of Joe's bucket. Rocks. It was filled with black beach rocks. It must have weighed a ton. Smothering a smile, Zachary returned to his work.

Joe claimed a stool near Gordon and clamped his hand on Gordon's shoulder, good spirits apparently restored. "It's good to see you, man."

Joe turned to Zachary and smiled. "I'm glad to see you again, too, Zachary. I hope you'll be staying with us at Inlet Beach for a long time."

Zachary could feel his face flush and he managed a quick 'thank you' before ducking his head again.

Joey opened the door for his mother, Maureen. She entered bearing a tray of thermoses and bags of marshmallows. Juliette followed, with bags of paper cups, napkins and plates.

After dumped everything on a side table, Juliette took the tray from her mother. "Should I set it up here?"

Maureen nodded. "Thank you, that would be great. Colleen is right behind me." She glanced at Joey. "Would you help Colleen, please?"

"I can manage a few boxes from the bakery." Colleen entered the room, the smell of warm bread following.

Zachary's stomach growled again.

Dilly leaned toward him and whispered. "The best stuff is in the green box. Joey made it himself and it's *epic*." She ducked her head and leaned closer. "I hid some, back at the beach house. When we go there later, I'll sneak you some."

Zachary looked for the green box that

Dilly was talking about. In the corner, someone had transformed a side table into a buffet. Over a bright red tablecloth and around bowls of cinnamon-scented pinecones were baskets of warm bread, platters of Christmas cookies, pitchers of cold milk and gallons of hot chocolate.

The room buzzed with conversation and laughter as the collection of beach ornaments grew. Every one of the decorations came from the ocean, the beach, or the dunes. There were sea grass wreaths studded with dried rose hips, perfectly round sand dollars hung from a snip of twine, tiny Christmas trees made from stacked driftwood pieces and topped with tufts of moss.

Zachary opened his heart and tucked this memory inside. Over the years, his collection of treasured Christmas memories would grow but this one – his first — would be his favorite.

Gordon rose from his stool with a groan and stretched. "I say we take a break. We can hang what we've got, come back and make more if we need to."

Joe laid down his pliers and sat back. "Charlie and Tyra should be here soon anyway. They got an early start and they're going to be hungry."

Maureen pushed back her stool. "Lydia's up at the beach house making lunch. I'll meet you up there."

The workroom door opened and Tyra entered, wearing one of Charlie's work coats cinched with a tool belt. A red scarf was wrapped nearly to her ears, and her nose was red with cold. Glancing around the room as she unwound her scarf, she found Zachary and smiled. "Hi Zachary. I hope I didn't wake you this morning. I tried to be quiet as I left."

Turning briefly, she tossed her hat and work gloves on the chair before walking toward him. "How are you feeling?"

She laid her cold hand on his forehead. Conversation in the room stilled and Zachary felt everyone's stare.

Before Tyra could answer, or report on Zachary's condition, Maureen squeezed in front of her. "Your hands are too cold. You're going to give him a chill."

Flicking Tyra's hand away, Maureen laid her own on his forehead. Her brows furrowed as she frowned. "You've left a cold spot, now I can't tell for sure if he's got a fever."

"Why don't you just ask the boy if he feels better?" Charlie entered the room talking, wearing a work coat and tool belt similar to Tyra's. Tugging a blue knit hat off his head, he looked at Zachary. "You feeling better?"

Zachary swallowed. "Yes."

Charlie raised both his hands in an exaggerated shrug. "See that? He's fine." With a quick wink at Zachary, Charlie pulled off his gloves and turned to Tyra. "Tyra, were you able to secure that last extension cord?"

Gordon interrupted before Tyra could answer. "You might want to keep those gloves on, Charlie. We're going up to the house for lunch."

Zachary watched from his stool as everyone rose and packed up the room. Garbage was tossed, food was boxed, and everyone talked at once. He was grateful for their help, and he understood they were busy, but a tiny part of him wished he was going with them. He couldn't, of course, because he still had to hang ornaments and find a way to repair the broken lights.

They left in small groups, talking and laughing, the same way they came in. As he watched them go, Zachary pushed his tears back — crying was for babies. They helped him make the ornaments, and that would be enough.

As he bent over his work, he heard the door open.

"Aren't you coming?" Charlie stood on the threshold, holding the door open.

Zachary snapped his head up. Hope sparked in his chest, but he pushed it away. "After I hang the ornaments, I need to fix the lights."

Charlie's smile was gentle. "We've already done that, Zachary. Tyra and I, early this morning. We saw you cleaning up and it made me proud. But you don't have to do everything alone, Zachary. Your family is allowed to help." He pointed to the center of the table, and Zachary noticed for the first time that the decorations everyone made were gone. "They're going to the tree, Zachary, but they won't hang anything without you."

Charlie moved toward him and gently pried the unfinished ornament from his fingers. "You've done enough."

And Zachary allowed himself to be led out the door and into his new home at Inlet Beach.

Thank you

There are so many people who have encouraged, inspired, and help shape this story. I am thankful for all of them.

For my critique group, a band of amazing writers who conjure magic every time they get together: Sandy Esene, Liz Vissner, Laurie Rockenbeck, Ann Reckner, Heather Stewart McCurdy, Bridget Norquist, and Michael Gooding. Your insights and encouragement have helped me more than you can imagine. Thank you.

For a group of stoic friends who read an early version of this story and provided detailed comments, in an impossibly short timeline: Sandy Esene, Liz Vissner, Laurie Rockenbeck, Colleen Broaddus, Mitch Patterson, and Barb Lutz. I'll give you more notice next time. — promise.

For Elisa Watkins, Allison Fletcher, Frances Carhart, Susie Woodard, Linda Harrower, and Debra Patterson. You are amazing, generous women and I'm fortunate to know you all.

For Beth Jusino, Jenn Reese, and Cindy Jackson. Fairy Godmothers for self-publishing. Your wealth of knowledge is immense and I am grateful to work with you. Thank you for keeping me sane.

For CMR: you will never know how much you've helped me.

For Hannah. Now that I'm finished, I can spend *all* my time with you. Aren't you a lucky kid?

And most importantly, for David. Thank you for making me believe I could write a second book. And thank you for cheering me on. You are the soap bubble on my pepper-water.

ABOUT THE AUTHOR

Heidi Hostetter currently lives in the beautiful Pacific Northwest with her family. They visit the beach every chance they get because you never know what will inspire a great story.

Connect with Heidi at www.HeidiHostetter.com, or find her on Facebook.

OTHER TITLES BY HEIDI HOSTETTER

The Inheritance

Book One of the Inlet Beach Novels

The house brought them together, but are the wounds of the past too deep for three sisters to reconcile?

Three estranged sisters learn they've inherited a dilapidated beach house from a relative they don't remember. The sisters each want something different from their unexpected gain.

PNWA 2015 Literary Contest Finalist
Available now on Kindle and wherever books are sold.

66305684R00091

Made in the USA
Lexington, KY
10 August 2017